Escape From Beaver Island

Escape From Beaver Island

By

Dr. Bo Wagner

Word of His Mouth Publishers
Mooresboro, NC

All Scripture quotations are taken from the **King James Version** of the Bible.

ISBN: 978-1-941039-63-2
Printed in the United States of America
©2025 Dr. Bo Wagner

Word of His Mouth Publishers
Mooresboro, NC
www.wordofhismouth.com

Chapter One

♪♪ "Well, the legend lives on from the Chippewa on down, of the big lake they call Gitche Gumee..."

I knew it was coming; we all did as soon as we saw the first billboard advertising the Great Lakes.

"The lake, it is said, never gives up her dead, when the skies of November turn gloomy."

Dad's voice was nasally as he did his best impersonation of some old singer/songwriter named Gordon Lightfoot.

"With a load of iron ore, twenty-six thousand tons more than the Edmund Fitzgerald weighed empty, that good ship and true was a bone to be chewed when the gales of November came early."

"Please tell me you aren't going to sing all seven thousand verses," Carrie moaned. She had her hand high on her forehead, and her eyes were squeezed tightly shut as if in agonized pain. But her plea fell on either deaf or determined ears; I knew this because Dad redoubled his efforts and his volume.

"The ship was the pride of the American side, coming back from some mill in Wisconsin. As the big freighters go, it was bigger than most, with a crew and good captain well-seasoned!"

"It really is a long song, Dad," I pleaded.

He showed some mercy; he didn't stop, but he did at least skip ahead a bit.

"When suppertime came, the old cook came on deck sayin', 'Fellas, it's too rough to feed ya;' at 7 PM, a main hatchway caved in, he said, 'Fellas, it's been good to know ya.' "

"Mommmmmmm! Make him stop!" Aly whined.

But he just ramped up his vocal efforts, seemingly determined to make us feel as if we ourselves were on board that ill-fated ship, sunk back in 1975 on Lake Superior.

"The captain wired in he had water comin' in, and the good ship and crew was in peril. And later that night, when his lights went outta sight, came the wreck of the Edmund Fitzgerald."

"Honey!" Mom finally shouted. Dad snapped out of his "performance brain" and glanced over at her as he drove.

"Yeah, babe?"

"I feel really bad for all twenty-nine brave sailors who went to a watery grave; I really do— but could we maybe just have the Tim Hawkins version instead?"

We all laughed, and then did it together at the top of our lungs:

"The story lives on how the boat she went down, and the people all died... bummer."

Yep, that's my family; not Tim Hawkins, he is just an awesome, clean comedian. No, my family is the five crazy people in a Yukon making their way up I-75 North heading for Michigan. Dad, who had just finished preaching a one-night youth meeting at the Emmanuel Baptist Church in Abingdon, a church I wrote about in Winter Wolf, was in the driver's seat. I could see his bright, smiling teeth gleaming out from under his mustache. Dad smiles a lot; he really seems to enjoy life and is always talking about how grateful he is to God for all of His blessings.

Mom, our audio savior at the moment, was beside him in the front seat, as always. She is, as he calls it, Beauty to his Beast, and the very heartbeat of our family.

Our family, by the way, is the Warners. I have already told you about Mom and Dad, but I should probably also mention that Dad is an evangelist and goes all over the place preaching, which is why we are always traveling somewhere with him.

There are three of us kids. I am Kyle, I am sixteen, and if I do say so myself, I am about as strong as a bull. Not as strong as Dad, though, at least not yet, but I plan on getting there one day. I am also six feet tall, which is way above average for a kid my age.

Carrie, age fourteen, who was breathing a sigh of relief from Dad no longer singing, is our resident genius. She is introspective, kind—and as sarcastic a human being as you could ever imagine meeting, when necessary.

Aly, the "please make him stop" whiner, is much more than that. My thirteen-year-old sister is brave, quick-tempered, deadly accurate with a slingshot, and sometimes as prototypical a blonde as any joke you have ever heard.

We kids, by the way, are something other than just the Warner kids.

We are the Night Heroes.

Why does God do what He does? Sometimes, the honest answer is, "I don't have a clue, but it sure is awesome." A few years ago, when my dad was preaching a meeting in Boomer, West Virginia, our lives as adventurers for the Lord started. We woke up to a call in the night and found ourselves awake in the broad daylight of West Virginia, a hundred years or more earlier. We had been brought there to rescue a brave little boy who had been captured by some bad men in a coal mine.

In that adventure, and all those to follow, we have learned that when we go to sleep in our time, we wake up in a previous time. But then, when we go to sleep in the past, we wake up in our time just as rested as if we had gotten a full night's sleep.

Whatever we go to sleep with, we can carry with us back into the past to help with whatever we need to do. And boy, has there been a whole lot of "needing to do!" We have fought Indians and whipped pirates and pounded slave owners and faced the Moth Man and a whole bunch more. And we always have only the five days that Dad is there to preach a meeting. On our last adventure, though, *The Sword and the Iron Curtain*, we unexpectedly had that cut down to just four days when Dad's meeting got shortened.

We got the job done, though, and we were still pretty amped up about all of it.

For now, though, we were firmly in the present. And the present was taking us to a place we had never been, Michigan. Specifically, we were going to the Oxbow Lake Baptist Church so Dad could preach a meeting for Pastor Chris Todd. He contacted us through a good mutual friend, Preacher Bryan Treadway.

We kids were really excited about this meeting; not only would we get to meet a bunch more new kids for us to be friends with, but we would also get to go across the border into Canada at some point during the week.

New state, new country!

Chapter Two

There really are no hotel options right there in White Lake, so it was the Holiday Inn in Waterford, ten minutes or so away from the church, whose parking lot Dad pulled into. We knew we would like it just from the looks of the outside; it was really pretty. In fact, we kids had all actually been surprised at how pretty the entire area was. I guess we kind of thought of "Detroit" when we were thinking of Michigan, but as it turns out, when you get outside of the big cities, Michigan is absolutely gorgeous. There are lakes, like, everywhere; it seemed like every other town we drove through was named after some lake or other. The trees were beautiful, and the leaves were turning vibrant colors. Honestly, it almost looked like God picked up a gigantic, big chunk of the South and put it up north and then decorated it with a ton of deep blue water.

As Dad had been on the phone with Pastor Todd on the way up, we could sort of overhear his voice on the other end. It was definitely a northern voice, but it was also really chipper, maybe even more so than Dad's. And one of the things we overheard a couple of times was "Lion's Den."

"That sounds absolutely delicious," Dad said at one point. I scrunched up my face and looked over at the girls, but their faces were already scrunched up as they looked over to me.

"The lions didn't get to eat Daniel," Aly whispered.

Carrie whispered back. "But they did get to eat the people who threw him in there. Maybe that's what he's talking about. What do you think, Kyle?"

"Not sure, Genius," was my own whispered reply, along with a confused shrug.

As it turns out, Dad and Pastor Todd were not talking Scripture; they were talking supper. We figured this out after we had gotten set up in our rooms, dressed for church, and back into the Yukon. The trip to supper was, like, two blocks. I grinned as we pulled into the restaurant and I saw the sign.

"The Lion's Den. Looks like in this one, the humans are the eaters instead of the eaten!"

And boy, did we eat. That place is GOOD!

But the fellowship was even better. We got to meet Pastor Todd and his wife, Mrs. Jennifer, and their three kids.

They were a good bit younger than us, but we really liked them. Their sons, Levi and Lincoln, are twins. Their daughter, Lydia, is as sweet as cotton candy. And they were, in Mom's words to us later that night, "very proper at the table." As she said this to us, she was sort of giving us the stink eye; I think maybe, for some reason, she feels like we need to up our manners game.

Rats: cute little kids were gonna get us into trouble.

We kids mostly sat around the table and listened as the adults talked. It was cool to hear Pastor Todd talk about the church and the area. White Lake is growing, and God seems to have brought Pastor Todd and the church together at just the right time for all of that.

Sadly, like all meals before a night service, we felt like it all ended too soon. But that was really okay with us, because every last one of us Warners love God more than anything and love to be in His house. And it was pretty obvious that the Pastor and his family felt the same way. So we cleaned up a bit at the table (no well-mannered kids should ever leave a mess for a waitress) and then headed to the vehicles. A few minutes later, we were pulling into the Oxbow Lake Baptist Church for our Saturday night through Wednesday night meeting.

Like a lot of what we had seen so far in Michigan, the church was really pretty. Not flashy or gaudy, but just genuinely beautiful.

As we walked inside, my eyes got wide, and I couldn't help but smile; we were greeted by some very familiar faces:

"Brother Josh!" my dad half-shouted, "you are a long way from Virginia!"

"Yes, sir, that I am. Enjoyed the good life, and now it is on to the even better life!"

We all laughed. Brother Josh and his wife, Mrs. Joanna, used to be on staff at the Emmanuel Baptist Church in Abingdon, the church we had just come from. They have three cute kids now, Preston, Colton, and Adley. We found out that he is now the assistant there at Oxbow.

Boy, being in the family of God means you meet family and friends all over the place!

We had about twenty minutes before the service to meet people, talk, and make new friends.

If you ever hear that people up north are not nice, don't believe it; if you meet the right ones, they will be some of the nicest people you ever get to know.

Right on the dot at 7 o'clock, Pastor Todd started the service. He quickly got Brother Josh into the pulpit, who then led us in a couple of lively congregational songs. I giggled a little bit as I saw people sort of looking back at us from time to time as we sang; we had to sound like human turnip greens to all of them with our southern accents!

There were some announcements, a couple of awesome special songs, and then Pastor Todd introduced my dad.

As Dad headed into the pulpit, there was something I didn't worry about in the least; I didn't worry whether or not he would be able to preach to people from a very different area of the country. I knew he could; not because of him, but because, as he always says, "The Word of God is the Word of God everywhere and for everyone; preach that, and you will be fine."

And he did. I could tell he was going a tiny bit slower than normal just to help people with non-southern ears to easily follow along, but other than that, he preached the exact same as always. And his first message to this new church for us was "Lay YOU At His Feet." It is from the middle part of the book of Ruth, one of my dad's favorite books to preach from. After Ruth had been working in Boaz's field for two months, Naomi instructed her on what to do to change everything. They had bills to pay, probably a lot of house repairs since the house had been vacant for years, and a thousand other needs. But rather than put a stack of bills or a stack of repair requests at the feet of Boaz, Naomi told Ruth to lay herself at his feet. And because she did that, the very next night, she was not Ruth, she was Mrs. Boaz, and all of her needs were forever met.

His point was that we always want to lay "stuff" at the feet of Jesus: bills, heartaches, family trouble, desires, and so much more. And while we are definitely supposed to cast all of our cares upon Him, like 1 Peter 5:7 says, the first and foremost thing we are all supposed to do is lay ourselves at His feet.

After the message ended, a lot of people were around the altar during the invitation doing just that.

We left the church really happy that night. We were looking back at a beautiful church and a parking lot full of friendly people, up at the beautiful Michigan sky dotted with a million twinkly points of light, and forward to a restful night's sleep.

Chapter Three

This was going to be good, and if Dad had been here, he would have been proud to the point of tears at what I was about to do.

"You sure about this?" the Conductor whispered.

"How many times has the shoe been very gleefully on the other foot, or feet, in this case?" I whispered back.

He pursed his lips and raised his eyebrows in an unmistakable "That's true" look.

I breathed in very deeply, gathering as much air as my lungs could possibly hold; if there were any dead nearby, I wanted to wake them, along with my sisters.

"JUUUUSSSSSSSSSSSST SIT RIGHT BACK AND YOU'LL HEAR A TALE, A TALE OF A FATEFUL TRIP, THAT STARTED FROM A TROPIC PORT ABOARD THIS TINY SHIP."

Carrie and Aly both screamed and looked like they were having their own personal rapture; I have never seen them get air like that! But I was not done with my sibling serenade:

"THE MATE WAS A MIGHTY SAILING MAN, THE SKIPPER BRAVE AND SURE, FIVE PASSENGERS SET SAIL THAT DAY FOR A THREE-HOUR TOUR, A THREE-HOUR TOUR..."

"Your weather is about to start getting rough, Kyle!" Carrie snapped angrily, paraphrasing the next line of the song that Dad had made sure we knew all too well. The Conductor doubled over with laughter; I had gotten my sisters good this time. I figured I was now only down by three or four in this long-running battle.

"I'm just glad the scenery is better than your singing," Aly grumped; she did not like being made to wake up when she still expected to be asleep.

The scenery really was nice. We were looking out at what could have been mistaken for an ocean, except for the fact that we could see land in the distance. The water was a deep, crisp, and lovely blue, and the breeze whistled across the lake and through the pines behind us.

Carrie and Aly were on their feet and beginning to compose themselves. They were also brushing the sand off their clothes; I had already done so.

"Well, this is something," Carrie said. "Not quite sure what yet, but something. Nice lakefront beach. No one shooting arrows at us. No snow or freezing cold; that one is definitely an upgrade over our last mission, no offense to Finland intended."

Aly took a quick look around and then gave her evaluation. "Looks kind of boring." Then she yawned the biggest yawn I had ever seen, with a Dad-level yawn noise to accompany it.

"Well, that was... a lot," the Conductor said with a wrinkly smile and a shake of the head. "Anyway, Carrie, I yield the floor to you for our traditional start to these things."

"Yeah, got it," she said as she looked around, taking it all in, "time and place. Let's start with place, since that's going to be the easy one here. We are on a pretty big island, but an island in the middle of a lake, not the middle of an ocean. That could be any one of a few, but based on the smaller islands I'm seeing around us, I'm going to go out on a limb and guess that we're on Beaver Island in Lake Michigan."

The Conductor just nodded ever so slightly, so she continued.

"When. Well, in our day, Beaver Island is both a permanent home to a few hundred people and a pretty hot tourist destination. So, based on the fact that there seem to be no hotels, no billboards, no planes overhead, nor any condensation trails from jets anywhere in the whole big blue sky, we are almost certainly pre-twentieth century, which could mean anything from the very dawn of creation to 1899.

"Best I can do with what I have to work with," she shrugged.

"You did well, as always," he beamed. "This is indeed Beaver Island, the largest of the islands in Lake Michigan. And the year is 1852."

He then paused a moment, spread his arms dramatically, and in a truly Shakespearean voice said, "Welcome to Zion, home of King Strang, ruler of Heaven and Earth!"

"Welp, maybe not quite so boring," Aly quipped.

I had a feeling she was right.

Chapter Four

"So, King Strange, seriously?" Carrie asked.

"Strang – get that one right," the Conductor said with mock seriousness. "The good king does not like being mislabeled, insulted, or even poked fun at."

"Cool!" Aly chirped. "We will be sure to do all of the above, then."

"I figured you might," he quipped. "But do not underestimate the man; he is a charismatic leader, and his most devout followers would do anything for him—and I do mean anything."

"Got it," I said simply. "So, who is he, and what makes him think he has the right to view himself as even an earthly king, much less a king that would dare use terms that only apply to King Jesus?"

"Excellent questions, Kyle. And, fortunately for you, I do have a few answers I can give you this time around. James Strang –"

Carrie interrupted. "Wait, what? King James? Like, the Bible?"

"That part is purely a coincidence," he shrugged. "James Strang is the leader of a splinter group of Mormons. After Joseph Smith died, he produced a letter supposedly from Smith stating that he was to be the new leader of the Mormons. Naturally, there was a power struggle over that, a power struggle that was won by Brigham Young. Most of the Mormons followed him to greener pastures in Utah. Strang, having lost most of his Mormon following, took the several hundred that were still loyal to him—they call themselves Strangites—and came here, to Beaver Island. They chased both the indigenous Ojibwe and Odawa peoples off the island and the Irish fishermen who lived and worked here as well.

"On July 8, 1850, Strang, leader of the Strangites, had himself coronated and crowned as 'King of Heaven and Earth.' And, since every king in his view needs a harem, he renounced his former opposition to polygamy and started 'marrying' a bunch of different girls and women."

"Ewwwwww, nasty," Aly growled.

"Not gonna argue with that," Carrie replied.

"So, we have a weirdo cult leader and his weirdo followers," I said as I scratched my head a bit, "but that still doesn't tell me why we are here.

I mean, if everyone is being weirdos by choice, that's on them. We can witness to them, obviously, but unless there's more, this just doesn't sound like a 'bring the Night Heroes' kind of problem."

The Conductor put both hands on my shoulder and looked directly into my eyes. "God does nothing by mistake, Kyle, you know that. And yes, there is more, but I have told you all that I am at liberty to say. The rest, some of which even I do not know, is up to you three to figure out. But I want you to trust me on something; I sense that you are taking this lightly, because in your words, Strang is just a 'weirdo cult leader' rather than a knife-wielding Indian or a giant wolf or a Moth Man. But the most dangerous people you will ever meet on this earth are those who do what they do in the name of the God that they do not really know. Strang is not to be underestimated, okay?"

"Understood, sir, and thank you," I said, and I meant every word of it. Good warnings are a gift, and listening to them can save lives and change outcomes.

The Conductor did not seem to have anything more to say, so I knew that it was time for us to get things started, and in the way we always did.

"Lord," I said slowly as my knees and those of my sisters touched the sand of Beaver Island, "here we are again at the start of another adventure. We thank You for giving us the privilege to serve like we do. And we thank You for giving us a good word of warning from the Conductor. I promise, we will not take anything lightly.

"We do not know who or what needs us, Lord. We do not know what we will be facing. But whoever and whatever, we do know that You are in charge. So, Lord, we offer ourselves to You again and ask You to use us, to keep us safe..."

"And to whack whoever needs whacking," Aly interjected.

"What she said, Lord," Carrie added dryly.

"You do see what I have to put up with, right, Lord?" I asked, stifling back laughter. "Amen," I was finally able to add.

And with that, the Night Heroes were officially on the job once again.

As we rose to our feet and brushed the sand off our knees, Aly cheerfully chirped, "So, bro, what do we need to know?" And then her eyes got wide, and she giggled, "Hey, I'm rhyming; I'm a poet!"

"No, Sweetie, just no," Carrie mildly lectured. Your rhyme would need rhythm and

26

meter to even begin to qualify as poetry; right now it is more 'NO-etry,' as in 'please stop that.' "

"Okkkaaaaaay," Aly clapped back sarcastically.

Carrie cut her eyes my way and said, "Letting her become a teenager was a bad idea."

I just shrugged, and said, "Walk and talk," as I motioned for them to follow me.

The day was lovely, and the air was clean; it was almost like breathing happiness. I motioned for the girls to come alongside me as we began to make our way slowly and quietly through the trees. They were hardwoods, mostly beech, sugar maple, and birch. The birds seemed undisturbed by our presence and continued their screeching and serenading from all around and above us.

"So, Carrie, our junior member here wants to know what we need to know. I can fill in at least part of that information; the Mormons are some of the nicest, most respectable, most harmless people you would ever want to meet. And yet, they believe very differently than what the Bible teaches about Jesus, about salvation, about a bunch of things, really. What other blanks can you fill in for us?"

"Well," she giggled, "you might want to mentally buckle up for this one, because it's a doozy. Ahem. The Mormons have as their founder a man named Joseph Smith. Let's go back to the year 1820. Joe Smith, as his neighbors in Palmyra, New York, knew him, supposedly had a vision in which God the Father and God the Son materialized and spoke to him as he prayed in the woods. They are supposed to have told him that They were most displeased by the current state of the Christian church in the world as it then was, and that They had chosen him to restore true Christianity."

"Wait, so, like, for 1800 years, there was no real Christianity, then?"

"Pretty much, Aly, yeah; at least according to Joe. In 1823, Smith supposedly had another vision. This time, he claimed that he was visited by an angel named Moroni."

"Moroni. An angel named Moroni. Seriously?"

"You are going to make this a very long story if you keep interrupting," I chided Aly, and Carrie took another breath and continued.

"Moroni was supposedly the glorified son of a man named Mormon, for whom the book and the religion are named. Moroni gave Smith the message that he was to receive the golden plates from which the doctrine of Mormonism would be received. The plates, according to Smith, were unearthed in the hills of Cumorah, New York. They were written in a language that does not exist, something he called 'Reformed Egyptian.'

A non-existent language called Reformed Egyptian; that one was funny, I thought, but I did not interrupt to say so, and Carrie continued.

"Well, since Joey boy did not know this fictitious language, Moroni supposedly provided him with an extremely large pair of 'magic glasses' to help him read it."

I had just taken a big swig of water; I immediately choked and spit it back out. I coughed a few times, finally caught my breath, and incredulously said, "Um, what? Did you really just say 'magic glasses'? You can't be serious."

"I am very serious, and so was Joseph Smith. The magic glasses were supposedly the Urim and the Thummim from the Old Testament priesthood. This, despite the fact that the Urim and Thummim were part of a breastplate and not a giant pair of 'magic glasses.' Through these magic glasses, Joseph Smith is said to have translated the book known as 'The Book of Mormon: Another Testament of Jesus Christ.' "

"Okay," I replied, "then that book is/was what Paul condemningly called 'another gospel given by an angel from heaven' in Galatians. Nice.

If Joseph Smith had known his Bible better, he might have thought of another story."

Carrie just nodded in agreement and then continued.

"Mormonism quickly gained steam among other small cultic groups, many of whom converted their entire congregations to Mormonism. In pretty short order, Joseph Smith told his followers of 135 direct revelations that he had supposedly been given by God, including one that began the Mormon practice of polygamy. This practice became so widespread among Mormons and so well known among the general public that the United States government threatened to confiscate all Mormon properties and dissolve their religious organization. Under such pressure, the 'divine revelation' given to Mormons by Joseph Smith was revoked in 1890 by new Mormon president Wilfrid Woodruff."

"So," Aly said as she wrinkled her face up, "Mormons can be very flexible with 'divine revelation from God' when they're getting in trouble for it."

"Yup," Carrie said simply, and then jumped in again. "Before that change, and as the Mormons began to grow and prosper in Illinois, their practice of polygamy became known to a local newspaper, who started writing about it and criticizing it. At this time in his creepy-culty career, Joseph Smith liked to be called 'The General.' Acting with 'righteous militant anger,' he destroyed the newspaper! For this, the state of Illinois imprisoned him and his brother Hyrum. On June 27, 1844, an angry mob stormed the jailhouse and killed Joseph and Hyrum, and Smith became a very unwilling martyr."

"We're getting pretty close to Strang time, then."

"Yes, Kyle, we definitely are. After Smith's death, the Mormons came under the control of Brigham Young, for whom the university is named. He is the one who beat out Strang for the gig. He led the Mormons to greater heights than Joseph Smith could have imagined. He was the one who, in 1846, led them on a brutal trek through the southwest to settle in the Salt Lake area of what would later become the state of Utah."

"Leaving Strang and his followers here to start their little kingdom on earth," I finished.

"Correct."

"Nice," I said simply. "Creepy cult leader dies, slightly less creepy cult leader gains control of most of the cult, extremely more creepy cult leader takes his splinter group from said creepy cult and starts an even creepier version of it here, on Beaver Island."

I turned to Aly. "So, got all of that, Pipsqueak?"

"I'm sorry, what? Who exactly are we whacking again?"

My head. That is what I whacked at that moment.

"Just follow along and pay attention, Squirt. We'll point you to your whack-ee when the time comes."

Chapter Five

Beaver Island is about thirteen miles long and six miles wide, making it roughly fifty-five square miles. We could tell right away that it was pretty much all flat; there was not a hint of mountains or even high hills anywhere.

"So, Kyle, we can't exactly just wander the length and breadth of the island at random; that would take a very long time. And since we have not been given any idea as to exactly where on the island the good king resides, what's your plan to find him in a reasonable amount of time?"

"That one will be pretty easy, I think, Carrie, and it doesn't really take a genius. Where will a true megalomaniac who calls himself 'King of Heaven and Earth' always be, no matter where he is?"

I saw Carrie grin, and she quickly replied, "Right in the center of everything."

"Bingo," I replied flatly. "Ten bucks says Megaloman has plopped his palace and throne right in the center of the island and has also built a nice high platform of some kind, from which everyone can see him and he can see everything in his 'domain.' "

We walked on in silence for a while, taking time to enjoy everything around us. It is pretty easy to get so busy *doing* that you don't take time for *being*, Dad always says. And anyway, if I was right about where Strang would be, we could cover the distance in less than half a day just by walking at a normal pace.

An island in the middle of a freshwater lake is sort of different from an island out in the Pacific somewhere. There were no palm trees swaying in the breeze, no monkeys, no coconuts, no pineapples, and no big, colorful birds. But there was a special beauty all its own just in the stately hardwoods stretching up toward the open expanse of the pale blue sky above and the leaves under our feet squishing like carpet beneath us.

Presently, we came up on a pretty cool treat.

"Apples!" I said with pleasant surprise. Sure enough, there was a clearly native apple tree, with plenty of fruit, ripe and fresh for the picking. We each grabbed a couple, then sat down at the base of the tree to enjoy a rest and a snack.

And it was in the middle of a "crunch" that I heard the "click."

I chewed that bite and swallowed slowly; Carrie and Aly did the same with theirs; we all knew that "click" sound very well.

I turned my head just a bit and saw two men, one maybe fifty-ish with a pot belly and droopy mustache, and the other very nervous one, probably in his twenties. That one had bug eyes that would have made a horse fly jealous. We had just been captured by Wilford "diabeetus" Brimley and Jim Varney (from the Earnest movies), apparently. Both were holding old-style rifles that I judged to be Sharps Model 1852s. They had them pointed our way—why does it always seem like someone is pointing a gun of some kind at us?

"Afternoon, Gents," I said pleasantly. "What can we do for you?"

"You can tell us why you, clearly strangers here, are eating the king's apples," the older one said with an unpleasant snarl.

"Well," I said slowly but calmly, "I judge this tree to be about forty years old. And if my information is correct, the king, as you call him, has only been on this island for three or four years. So, I would say these apples belong to the King who made Heaven and Earth, not any earthly king, and we just so happen to be the children of that King."

"Don't spout your heresy to me, boy!" he shrieked. "There is but one king, and he will call you to answer for stealing from him."

"Great!" Aly chirped. "That means you'll take us to him, right? Cause, like, we don't feel like wandering around looking for him if there is an easier way."

"Silence, girl!" he hissed. "In this kingdom, your kind is to be seen, not heard; is that clear?"

I could see Aly bristling up; this dude was going to have himself a pretty serious problem before this adventure was over, of that I had no doubt. For now, though, I needed to calm things down; we really did need to go ahead and get to Strang.

"Easy, there, sir," I said politely. "We didn't mean to offend you or to eat anyone's apples without permission. What say you go ahead and take us to your boss, if that is okay with you; we would actually very much like to speak to him."

He just nodded to the left with his head, the gun still pointing directly at us. We knew what he meant, so we all rose slowly to our feet and started walking toward the pathway through the trees that he indicated with that nod of the head.

Without even having to say it, the order of our trek was Aly out front, Carrie behind her, and me behind them. This put me between them and the guns pointing at our backs. Dad raised me right; men are to put themselves in between danger and others, and I would not have it any other way.

The pathway was not hard to follow; it is exactly the way we would have gone with or without those Sharps 1852s prodding us. As we walked, I was actually kind of chewing myself out a bit; I should have been expecting there to be sentries keeping watch all over the island. But because we were dealing with "just a creepy cult" instead of Indians or pirates, I let my guard down. The Conductor's warning had not gotten far enough through my thick head, apparently.

Presently, the path took a turn to the right, and I grinned and shook my head as all of our feet started to clopity-clop along; we were now walking on bricks that had been painted gold.

"I see the good king has himself an, um, 'street of gold,' " I said as seriously as I could. "Wherever did he get that idea?" I said over my shoulder to our captors. "I don't remember that in the Book of Mormon."

"Some things in the Bible happen to be correct," he said condescendingly.

Some things. Yep, that was a pretty good explanation of how cults get started to begin with. Take away a perfect final authority, and anything goes, I guess.

Maybe half a mile later down the Temu version of the street of gold, we came up on what I could only assume was the "gates of pearl." They were clearly wooden, mind you, but someone had done an admirable job of painting them a nice, shiny, pearlish color.

"It's a lot less than what I've always been expecting," Carrie quipped.

"Shut up, girl!" Earnest shrieked. "No one insults the city of the great king!"

As we made our way through the gates, a crowd began to gather around—and it was a sad sight, really. It only took me a couple of seconds to size it all up. Old men: unsuccessful, past their prime, frustrated with life, now relishing in the attention of a "king." Young men: socially awkward, frustrated, brought into the fold like religious gang members. They had doubtless been promised the world and bought the whole bit, hook, line, and sinker. Women: part one; weak-minded pushovers who believed every word their cult leaders said and would go to their graves never wavering, no matter what. Women: part two;

young ladies and young girls who clearly did not want to be there. Their faces were etched with fear that I could feel in my bones, but their wills had mostly been broken.

Those, those were the ones that we were there for.

Chapter Six

"Move along, urchins," Wilford demanded, and we did. The "kingdom" was basically a huge, semi-circle village, facing the gates we had just come through. Everything was neat, organized, and so perfectly spaced as to make a person with hyper-OCD jealous. And, just as I had suspected, in the center of it all was a clearly man-made "mountain" about twenty feet tall, with an elaborate (for their day) structure on the very top.

"The mountain of God!" Earnest said reverently.

She did it so quickly I could not stop her. In her best "Hulk from the Avengers" voice, Carrie quipped, "Puny God."

Screaming, Earnest bolted from the rear of the line to attack her—and met my forearm, neck high, as he rushed that way. My clothesline sent him into a full backward flip, and he landed flat on his face, out like a light.

It was instant chaos; Wilford tried to raise his weapon, but I caught the barrel with my left hand and laid him out with my right. I knew this was not going to end well for us, though; Strang's followers were rushing out of every nook and cranny, and all of them had murder in their eyes.

My sisters and I formed a triangle, back-to-back-to-back, and got ready for one last stand. How weird that we had survived Nazis and Indians and wolves and pirates and the Moth-Man and were now going to die at the hands of *Little House on the Prairie* meets Jim Jones zombies!

And then it all instantly stopped. The word had been spoken calmly and quietly, yet everyone was so attuned to his voice that they all heard and obeyed without hesitation.

It had merely said, "Peace."

The scene was surreal, to say the least. There, on the perch of his palace, was a man who looked to be in his mid-thirties. His right hand was outstretched as if reaching down to his followers. He had a full, rounded beard, a full head of hair despite a slightly receding hairline, and eyes so blue that they almost shone. He was smiling, and it seemed so incredibly genuine. Overall, he looked like the most pleasant, likable person in the entire world.

"Not what I was expecting," I heard Carrie whisper.

"Nope," I replied. I was very much used to pounding slimy slave owners and knife-wielding Indians and other bad guys that looked like, well, 'bad guys.' This guy looked like how a modern artist would probably mistakenly portray Jesus.

"Welcome, guests," Strang said pleasantly. "My apologies for such an unpleasant reception."

Then, as he turned to go back into his palace, he said, "Bring them to me." I could have sworn that, in that brief second, his voice became way, way more sinister.

The room was all in very smooth wooden planks, floor, walls, and ceiling. There were flowers in every corner, and the curtains were lovely and clearly very expensive. Most notable of all, though, there was a large portrait of Strang himself just right of center on the wall to our left. He was dressed in royal robes, holding a golden scepter, and wearing a huge, bejeweled crown.

This dude clearly thought a lot of himself.

In the kitchen area, tea was steeping pleasantly, being attended to by a girl who seemed to be in her late teens. Carrie was inhaling the air, loving the smell of chamomile and mint.

"Bring them the tea, please, Esther," Strang said.

Carrie sniffed the air again.

Don't get complacent, Sis, I was thinking to myself, somehow hoping she would get the message. Strang was mulling about, gathering some pastries from the counter, and once the platter was full, he set it in front of us, and then sat down himself.

"I had forbidden the use of tea when I was in Wisconsin," he said pleasantly. "The Word of Wisdom encourages abstinence from such. However, here in my new kingdom, we are a bit more relaxed on such matters. We want everyone to enjoy their stay here as we work to spread the kingdom across the earth from this point."

Strang took a sip of his tea, and by that point, the young lady was bringing all of ours to the table as well. She handed one to Carrie, the next to Aly, and the last to me. We each thanked her, and yet, both of my sisters looked at me out of the corners of their eyes.

I nodded ever so slightly, and we all sipped ours as well. I was figuring that there had clearly not been time for any poison to be prepared, since our coming was not known, and that, if Strang had wanted us dead, he would have simply let his disciples finish the job down in the courtyard.

Strang did not miss that subtle cue.

"You are wise to look to your elder, young ladies; there is wisdom in years, especially in the years of men."

I could see Aly starting to bristle up again; she was going to whack somebody for sure before this day was done if I did not get her reigned in.

Strang must have seen the same thing and not wanted that as of yet. I had to give him credit, he definitely knew how to work a room.

"How did such lovely young ladies end up following this brute of a brother to my kingdom anyway?" he asked them. His smile was radiant; this guy could sell toothpaste to a basketball.

"Oh, you know," Carrie began, "we just wanted to see the sights, and this island seemed like such a pretty place, we just had to come over and check it out. And we always travel together; our folks would not have it any other way."

"Then your parents are wise," Strang said more seriously. "This world is growing ever darker, and until the light shines across it, no one will be truly safe."

"What light?" Aly asked in her most innocent voice. I was glad that, for the moment, she was sticking to the task rather than instigating trouble. We really needed to figure out what this whole situation was about and what made this guy tick.

Strang got up from the table and walked to the window of his wooden and thatched palace. We could feel the breeze blowing in; the window was merely an opening, with louvers that could be closed if any storms blew in. He stood there for a moment with his hands clasped behind his back as if in contemplation. Then, as he spoke, I could have sworn it was another voice entirely than the one we had been hearing; it was really eerie, that. Making it even more unusual was that after just a couple of lines, we realized he was speaking in poetry.

> "Long hath man been bound to
> Earth, with Earth's now faded
> glory,
> Long the time since truth was
> heard, to sing the joyful story.
> For man was ne'er designed to be
> a fleeting, dying thing,
> Nor was he made to wander far,
> while longing for a king.
> The days have come when all this
> wrong will surely be made right,
> And I am sent to lead my people
> safely to that light."

His voice trailed off, and all was silent for several seconds.

Then Strang abruptly turned to us again, and was back in his normal voice, with an extra dose of "cheer" seemingly added to it.

"So, you wanted to see lovely Beaver Island, and you have now seen it. You have met my people, misunderstandings have been resolved, and all is well. You have enjoyed my tea—and hopefully, my poetry—and now I must send you off. I have much business to attend to here, many people who depend on me, and I must fulfill my responsibilities. I assume you came to my island by boat, since you have neither feathers nor wings. So please be careful on your way back to shore, and on your trip back across the water to the mainland.

"And, at the risk of sounding rude, please do not come back to Beaver Island; while we do not mind extending hospitality to Gentiles, hospitality taken advantage of leads to resentment. Goodbye, children."

And with those words, he turned and walked out of the palace, and two large men that we did not even know were there came in off of the back porch, lifted their hands toward the front door, and we knew we were being ushered out.

The men left us at the beginning of the yellow brick road, as I called it. Then, as they turned to go back to the compound, one shouted over his shoulder, "See that you do not delay to leave."

"Will do, as soon as it gets dark," Carrie whispered. Aly and I nodded in agreement, and we made our way back toward the shore. No, we did not have a boat, but we knew that we did have our standard nightly "sleep ride home" waiting for us.

A couple of hours later, we were hunkered down under a makeshift lean-to and ready to go to sleep/go back to our time.

"Well, I would say we still have no idea what any of this is about," Carrie said with mild annoyance. "Other than bad poetry and worse theology, it really doesn't seem like Strang is guilty of much."

I leaned back a bit farther, reached into my pocket, and pulled out a tiny slip of folded paper.

"Wanna bet?" I said simply.

"What's that?"

"This, my genius sister, is the piece of paper that Esther slipped to me under my cup of tea."

Their eyes got really wide.

"Whadda ya wanna bet it says something like 'get me out of here'?" I asked as I opened it.

I was close; very close. As Carrie and Aly looked over each of my shoulders, we all saw the words, "Please help me! Velora."

Chapter Seven

The sheets felt good, the pillow felt good, the morning felt good. Man, I really do love life, especially this life God has given us as PKs, preacher's kids. We would get to enjoy being in church most all day on this beautiful Sunday and would also doubtless get to go see some local sites in the afternoon.

"Why did she sign it 'Velora'?" Carrie asked from their side of the room. "I mean, it's a cool name; it is from the Latin word that means valor. But Strang clearly called her Esther."

"Just guessing, here," I said, "but I would say that Velora is her real name. Esther in the Bible had a real name as well, Hadassah. It was changed when she was brought into the palace. I'm guessing that Strang did the same thing with Velora. Esther means 'a star,' and I'm just guessing that she is his 'star,' whether she wants to be or not."

"Ewww," Aly said through a half yawn. "Do you mean what I think you mean?"

"If you think I mean that Strang kidnapped that girl and that she is being held against her will as part of his unholy harem, then yes, that is exactly what I think."

"Man, this day needs to hurry up and end, then, so I can totally desicate this dude," she said angrily.

I just looked at her, trying to make sense of that. Carrie, though, figured it out pretty quickly.

"Um, to 'desicate' means to dry something out. Do you by chance mean 'decimate,' to completely destroy?"

"Yeah, that, demiscate!"

Carrie and I just shook our heads and let it go.

Half an hour later, we were all ready and down in the hotel lobby, having a quick bite of breakfast.

"Sleep well?" Mom asked with her typical cheerfulness.

"Pretty well," Aly said, "but I did have some Strang dreams."

I nearly spit out my orange juice, but Mom and Dad, fortunately, completely missed that quip.

A bit later, we were all piled into the trusty old Yukon one more time and heading over to the Oxbow Lake Baptist Church. It didn't take long to get there, and there was already a decent crowd of cars in the parking lot when we pulled in.

As we exited the vehicle and headed into the church, people greeted each other and us. We made our way inside and pretty quickly figured out where our various Sunday school classes were.

An hour later, we were all back in the auditorium for service. The congregation began to sing, and like Bible-believing churches everywhere, the words were filled both with worship and theology. It is hard to imagine a better way to get your heart in tune to the preaching of the Word of God than to sing of how wonderful He is and of the truths of His Word.

After some special singing, Pastor Todd called Dad up to the pulpit, and Dad had everyone open their Bibles to Hebrews 11:5. That verse is about a really cool character and true story from the Old Testament, Enoch, the guy who walked with God and got to walk straight into Heaven without even dying. But the main thing Dad pointed out about him was that before he left Earth, in the middle of a totally wicked world, Enoch had a testimony that he pleased God. Everybody no doubt hated him, but everybody also freely admitted that Enoch was a good and a godly man.

The title of his message was "The Treasure of a Good Testimony."

I really, really hope I am doing a good job of building a good testimony like Enoch; I would hate for anyone to watch me and decide that Jesus really isn't worth following.

The message seemed to go over really well, and people came to the altar to pray during the invitation. Then the pastor closed the service, and it was on to lunch, or as I call it, "one of my three favorite meals of the day."

Our family, the pastor and his family, and Brother Josh and his family all went to a place called the Highland House, and it was really good; Michigan apparently knows how to cook! Some of us got burgers (which were huge), others got salads (which were also huge), and some of the adults got other things like chicken or steak.

We laughed, talked, ate, and just had a general, all-around great time. As I have heard my dad say so often, God's people may not be perfect, but you will find that they are the best people on Earth!

Once we finished lunch, we said our goodbyes and then went for a drive. We didn't have any place in particular in mind, and that didn't really matter; just about everywhere you go up there has some amazing-looking lake to drive around.

After an hour or so of driving, we headed back to the hotel and got a little bit of rest ahead of the night service. Then it was back into the Yukon and back over to the Oxbow Lake Baptist Church.

The night service was just as sweet as the morning service and almost as well attended. As in the morning, the singing was from the heart, and our southern twang voices meshed with the voices of our northern brothers and sisters in Christ, and I knew the sound had to be lovely in the ears of the Lord.

Finally, it was time for Dad to get up and preach once again. This time, the message was both humorous and pointed. It was one of Dad's newer messages that goes by the title, "You'll Be Sorry!" It is about the time when John the Baptist confronted Herod over a pretty icky sin. He had taken his brother Philip's wife. Worse still, she was niece to both of them! Anyway, when John confronted Herod, Herod put him in prison. He really wanted to kill him, but he was afraid to do so because the people regarded John as a prophet. Sometime later, though, Herod's wife sent her daughter to do a dirty dance for him and his creepy friends.

Herod promised to give her whatever she wanted. And her mama had already given her the answer: she wanted John the Baptist's head on a charger, a gigantic plate.

So, Herod beheaded John. He got what he wanted, right? But the Bible says, "and he was sorry." As it turns out, Herod figured out too late that people who will always tell you what you want to hear are a dime a dozen, but people who will tell you what you need to hear are irreplaceable.

I have some people like that: Mom and Dad. I made up my mind then and there that I would always be grateful for them telling me the things I need to hear, even if I don't like what they are telling me.

Just like in the morning, there was a good response around the altar once again. And then the service concluded, we all said our goodbyes for the night, and we headed to the hotel.

And I was already thinking of ways to make James Strang very, very sorry.

Chapter Eight

The "boom" was so loud that all three of us jumped up like we thought we had missed the Rapture. My immediate (very weird) thought was that a trash truck had picked up a metal dumpster in the parking lot and dropped it. Carrie later said that she thought a gas leak had blown up the hotel, and Aly thought a war had broken out and bombs were being dropped.

As it turns out, she was the closest to what was really happening.

"Move! Move!" the Conductor shouted over the next boom. Instantly, we were on our feet and running. We did not know exactly where we were or where we were running to, but as I heard the next shrill whistle followed by another deafening boom, I knew that cannons were being fired—and that we were in the line of fire.

A cannonball landed maybe thirty yards off to our left, and all of us were knocked off of our feet by the blast and went tumbling into the bushes.

My ears were ringing badly; I tried to shake the cobwebs out of my head as I looked around for Carrie and Aly and the Conductor.

I found them. Carrie was doubled over in a fetal position; the blast had knocked the breath out of her. Aly had gotten back up and was rushing toward her. The Conductor, though, was clearly not hurt at all. I figured that may be important for me to remember; it sort of confirmed what we three had long thought about him. He rushed over to Carrie, helped her up, and Aly joined him on Carrie's other side. She was limping a bit, but together, Aly and the Conductor helped her to cover under the trees.

I joined them, then looked around to take stock of our position and situation.

It was a small town. Wooden buildings that fit the time period. Middle of the night. Some of the buildings were on fire. I could see the outline of the shore in the distance; we were on the mainland, and out there in the water somewhere was Beaver Island. I had a strong hunch that the good king was here rather than there, though, and in a few seconds, my suspicions were confirmed.

"Look!" Aly hissed. Sure enough, amongst other men now storming into the town, there was James Strang, pointing and barking orders.

"There, the general store. Liberate all the supplies from these Gentiles; the kingdom needs them."

Even though my head was still spinning, and I was starting to get nauseous for some reason, it clicked with me in that moment that the day before, Strang had called us Gentiles. That was weird; he and his people were obviously Gentiles as well. I made a mental note of that—and then threw up.

"Be still, Kyle," Aly said as she knelt beside me. "I am guessing the blast busted an eardrum for you, which is making you dizzy and sick."

"Thanks, junior nurse-in-training," I whispered between heaves. All sarcasm aside, she would be a good nurse one day. God built her that way.

I was mad, helpless, and mad because I was helpless. Strang and his men were stealing supplies, hurting people, and, from the screams of girls that I was hearing, probably adding to his unwilling harem as well. Man, did the Conductor's warning from yesterday feel like a baseball bat to my head at that moment; he was right, and we way underestimated James Strang.

"We need to do something," Carrie said as she stood up and tried to move forward. But she took just one step before she winced in pain and backed up into the trees again.

"Wow, some heroes we are," Aly said sadly. "This sure seems like a gigantic loss for Team Night Heroes."

The din was starting to die down; Strang and his men had hit hard and fast and were now making for the shoreline and their boats to go back to their kingdom.

The Conductor put a fatherly arm around Aly.

"Losses come in two forms, young lady: those that put your fire out, and those that add fuel to it. And that is entirely dependent on you. So, what will it be? There are people who need help, and the King, the real King, trusted you to bring that help. Was He wrong?"

"He is never wrong, sir," I answered weakly, though the question was directed to Aly. "But I just don't know how much use we will be at this point; we are pretty banged up."

He nodded, then said, "Good."

I knew what he meant, and I knew that Carrie and Aly did, too. How many times had we heard Dad preach it? Like God told Paul when Paul had a thorn in the flesh, His strength is made perfect in our weakness.

Maybe we—no scratch that—maybe I, me, Kyle, had gotten confident in my size and strength.

God gives us gifts like that, but we humans so often turn around and place our confidence in those gifts rather than in the God who gave them. Whenever Israel did that, God let them take a loss to remind them to trust Him.

"Got it, sir," I said. I took a deep breath, stood up slowly, and surveyed the scene. Wow, just wow; the place was a wreck, and there did not seem to be any life anywhere.

"With the Lord's help, we will be back tomorrow," I said, "bumps and bruises and all. And we will use whatever gifts and abilities from God that we still have to rescue whoever we can rescue, and to deal with James Strang."

"Good," he said. "A good night of sleep will do wonders for all of you, though you will definitely not be one hundred percent for a while."

"No biggie, my guy," Aly chirped cheerfully, "With God's help, seventy percent Night Heroes will still be enough to whack old Jimmy Cracked Cornball and rescue the damsel."

We laughed—and I passed out.

Chapter Nine

I slept fitfully, but I slept. When my eyes started to blink open in the morning, though, I could feel the nausea starting to build again.

Aly was already beside me, ready for that.

"Here, Kyle, eat some of these pretzels. The salt will help settle your stomach."

I nodded, took a few from the little snack bag she was holding in front of me, and popped them in my mouth as I sat up. I chewed and swallowed, and she handed me a cup of water to wash it all down with.

"Carrie?"

"In the bathroom, getting ready," she said. "She is fine; she just had the wind knocked out of her for a bit."

"You?"

"Been better," she shrugged. "Got a bit of a limp, but not as bad as Carrie; I hope Mom and Dad don't notice either one."

I nodded, then got up. This hotel room had a sink by the fridge, so I brushed my teeth and used some mouthwash; my mouth felt really nasty from last night, and I kind of shuddered when I remembered why.

The bathroom door opened, and Carrie, all ready for the day, stepped out.

"All yours. You good?"

"Ehh," I answered. Then I got my clothes and stuff and headed in there for a long, hot shower.

It was a good chance to pray and to think, and I spent a while doing both.

As the warm water washed over me, I thought about those captives on Beaver Island. They were in the worst kind of predicament: captured and tormented by those who commit their evil in God's name. It made me furious on two levels. One, I hate bullies, and two, I hate it when anyone behaves like a jerk and makes God look bad in so doing.

I finished my shower, dried off, got dressed, and turned the restroom over to Aly, who followed suit.

A little while later, we joined Mom and Dad in the hotel lobby for breakfast. I took the stairs down there slower than normal; my balance was off, and my hearing was at maybe sixty percent.

"Morning, sleepyheads!" Dad said cheerfully. "Guess what day it is?"

"Um, Monday?" Aly replied with a wrinkled brow.

"You could call it that. You could also call it Canaday; today, we will be heading across the northern border!"

Cool; very cool.

We chowed down on pancakes, waffles, and fresh fruit while Mom and Dad told us what we could likely expect for the day. She also reminded us that we would need both passports and good manners; we did not need any shenanigans while crossing the border into another country.

When we finished breakfast, we cleaned everything up, hopped in the trusty old Yukon, and headed over to the church. Pastor Todd and his whole family would be coming with us, and all of us would be riding in the church van together.

The day was perfect for an excursion; puffy white clouds flitted across an impossibly blue sky, and there was just the faintest hint of coolness in the air.

It took a while to get everyone into place, but finally, all seats were secured and/or belts buckled, and we were headed out.

We were on Highway 59 for a little while, then onto I-75 heading for Detroit. When Dad saw the sign with that name, I heard him say, "Mo-town..."

I had a bad hunch I was about to find out what that meant. Sure enough...

♪♪ "I've got sunshine on a cloudy day; when it's cold outside, I've got the month of May..."

And then, of all things, Pastor Todd joined in with him as both his wife and our mom rolled their eyes. "I guess you'd say, what can make me feel this way? My girl, my girl, my girl, talkin' bout, my girl, my girl!"

Now all of us kids were rolling our eyes, too. I was actually kind of glad, at that moment, that I still was not hearing too well.

Mercifully, the serenade ended soon enough. And about forty-five minutes later, we were coming into Detroit, a first for us.

For some reason, I guess I always had it in my mind that the border of the U.S. and Canada was a whole bunch of trees and wilderness. As it turns out, it is actually a whole lot of steel and pavement instead, with the wide and deep Detroit River running between them. Michigan is on this side; Windsor, Ontario, is on the other. And as it turns out, you can either go over or under the river to get from one side to the other; the Ambassador Bridge will take you over, and the Detroit/Windsor tunnel will take you under.

We chose "over" for the trip in.

Before we could go over, though, we had to go through border security. No sensible nation just lets people walk or drive right in; good governments protect their citizens by making sure they know every single person that crosses the border and know that they are not going to do any harm.

Once we got through that, crossed the river, and parked, we all piled out and then headed down to the river walk and sculpture park. Carrie's limp was so slight that Mom and Dad either had not noticed it or did not say anything about it, and I was glad for that.

As for the river walk and sculpture garden, it was really cool:

From there, we headed into the Chimczuk Museum. That was pretty cool, too; it was especially fun to see the displays of how things were a bit different from America to Canada, and the display on how the tunnel was built.

Once we were done at the museum, we had lunch at Thyme Kitchen. That was really good; my chicken panini was excellent. And then we found a gift store and got some Canadian souvenirs.

For most kids, a river walk and a museum and lunch and a gift store may not seem like an exciting day; for us, especially since we love being with our folks and our friends and love seeing and learning new things, it was awesome.

Way too soon, though, we had to start heading back. Dad would want some time to gather his thoughts and pray before service, and we all needed to do a little schoolwork. So we headed back to the van and, this time, we made the return trip under the river and through the tunnel, once again going through border security—this time, American border security.

Detroit quickly began to fade into the distance behind us, and I leaned my head on the van window and watched the sky as we traveled. I got to go to a new place today, Canada. But one day I would get to go to an even way cooler place up there past those clouds and that blue sky, a place called Heaven, and I would never have to leave once I got there.

And it would not cost me or my parents anything. In the words of a hymn that we all love to sing, "Jesus paid it all." Man, anyone who does not know Him as their Savior does not know what they are missing!

I nodded off with that happy thought bouncing around in my brain. Normally, I don't fall asleep while riding in a vehicle; I guess my body knew I needed some healing time.

Chapter Ten

"Wake up, Twinkie; what's the matter? Did you do too much running and playing in your dreams last night?"

My eyes popped open at Dad's voice; I am just glad my mouth did not pop open and say something inadvisable in response to his question!

I stretched and could sort of hear buckles unsnapping and doors opening. So, I unbuckled myself and wiggled my way out of the van to join the others.

We said our temporary goodbyes and loaded up into the Yukon to head back to the hotel. Those miles passed pretty quickly, and soon we were in our two rooms, either studying, working, or resting, depending on who we were and what was needed. And then, quicker than we would have thought, we were getting dressed for church yet again.

"Move it, move it, move it, Sluggards!" Dad was barking cheerfully. "'Tis time for sustenance yet again!"

Sustenance: only Dad and Carrie used big words like that for "supper."

Sustenance, by the way, was a Culver's before church. In case you don't know, Culver's is a not-quite-fast-food place that started in Wisconsin but is now spreading down even into the South. They are famous for their cheese curds, which sounds terrible, but tastes delicious. Their butter burgers are also, in Mom's words, "to die for."

After supper, it was back over to the church for the most important part of the day.

The service started with lovely, heartfelt singing once again:

"Alas, and did my Savior bleed, and did my Sovereign die? Would he devote that sacred head for such a worm as I...

"At the cross, at the cross, where I first saw the light, and the burden of my heart rolled away! It was there by faith I received my sight, and now I am happy all the day..."

I don't remember the songs after that; they were great, and I sang them, but my heart and thoughts were really stuck on that "the burden of my heart rolled away" part. I still remember when I realized I was a sinner and asked Jesus to forgive me and save me; I have never felt ay better a second in my life than at that moment when all my burdens rolled away.

I guess I zoned out thinking about all of that, because I snapped back to attention the moment Pastor Todd called Dad up to preach once again. This time his message was *Beauty Where The Blood Fell.* It is about the day Jesus was crucified, and especially about the four ladies and one man who made it to the foot of His cross to be with Him in His darkest hour. They were right there in the middle of all the ugly, and that made their devotion all the more beautiful.

Dad's point was that any of us can be beautiful for the Lord when everything is going well; that is really easy. But what really makes a difference is when we can be beautiful for God even when it seems like our whole world is falling apart.

"I want to be like that," Carrie whispered into my one good ear.

I just nodded; I did too.

The invitation was productive, with a lot of people at the altar again.

Twenty minutes later or so, we were back in the Yukon, heading for the hotel and a night of sleep for Mom and Dad, and a rematch with James Strang for the Night Heroes.

Chapter Eleven

The gentle waves lapping up onto the shore were an excellent way to wake up; way better than all the booming and crashing and screaming from last night. I rolled over, sat up, and brushed the sand from the beach off my shoulder.

Carrie and Aly were still asleep on either side of me.

"So, how are you feeling today?"

I looked up at the Conductor; he was facing the water but clearly knew that I was now awake.

"Better than last night, sir. Definitely still out of balance, but I'm adjusting."

He nodded. "Your balance has served you well many, many times; I do not think you would have wanted to face Black Crow without it."

"Nope," I said simply. "But, wobbly or not, I still need to deal with Strang. Got any advice on that? I mean, other than the advice I already ignored, like a dork?"

"Weeellllll, I think Kyle has made some excellent progress today."

Carrie was now clearly awake, and I had to admit, her impression of Violet from *The Incredibles* was spot on.

The Conductor grinned. "Nice, Carrie, very nice. And as to advice, Kyle, no, I have no advice. I do, though, have a bit of information that may come in handy, if you are interested."

"Yes, sir, I'm interested. What do you have?"

"Only this. Those supplies taken from the Gentiles last night—"

I interrupted.

"Excuse me, sir, I apologize for interrupting, but since you mentioned it, I have to ask about that Gentile thing before I forget to do so. Strang keeps using that word, and now you just used it. But all of us, including Strang, are Gentiles. So, what's up with that?"

"Ahh, yes, the Gentile thing; sorry about that, I should have already explained. Strang holds an even weirder view of Replacement Theology than the already weird, 'normal' Replacement Theology."

"Replacement Theology? I've heard Dad talk about that. That's when Christians think God has replaced the Jews with them, right? And all the promises He made to the Jew are now theirs?"

"Correct, Kyle. Now, clearly, that is unbiblical nonsense. But Strang has made that nonsense even more nonsensical. He believes that his splinter group of Strangites has not only replaced the Jews, but that those Jews, and all Christians other than his decidedly non-Christian cult that thinks they are Christians, are now Gentiles, and that he is now basically Christ Himself."

Carrie and Aly both stared "that stare" at him, the stare that our generation has mastered so well.

"Yes," he said in response to their stare, "it is stupid."

I shook my head, trying to clear this new layer of cobwebs. "So, how does that information help us?"

"It doesn't, yet; you interrupted me, remember?"

"Ahh, yeah, my bad, sir. Please, proceed."

He nodded. "As, *ahem,* King of Heaven and Earth, the good 'king' has built himself a harem to enjoy; he even added to his number of concubines last night. But a king must have a queen, and he has chosen his."

"Did he bother to even ask her?" Aly said, and I could hear the anger in her voice and see the fire in her eyes as she did. I suspected she was not going to get any less angry when she heard the answer.

The Conductor smiled, and his face was both kind and a bit sad, all at once.

"No, young lady, he did not. The 'king' does as he pleases, and asks permission of no one."

Carrie's words were slow and deliberate. "Let me guess; Velora?"

He merely nodded.

"When?"

"Three days from now, Carrie, three days from now. As I was saying a moment ago, those supplies taken from the Gentiles last night were for a wedding and to furnish an even grander island palace for Strang. Velora will be his queen, and if she crosses him, well, it will go badly for her."

I could feel anger rising through every part of my body; I was going to hurt James Strang, very, very badly. A king? Yeah, no. America has never had a king—or has she? Apparently, there was indeed a king, at least on Beaver Island. But this king was neither noble nor nobility. This king was a common thief with enough charisma to turn his own hijacked cult into a monarchy. And he and his followers did a great job of "appropriating supplies from the nearby Gentiles" to keep their little kingdom running well.

They did an equally great job of keeping people in the fold, even when they no longer wanted to be there, and even when they were going to have to marry into the creepy king's harem.

As it turns out, God has a solution for that kind of thing.

A three-member, rough and tumble, always looking for a fight solution called the Night Heroes.

A few moments later, we Night Heroes were getting up off our knees. We intended to put James Strang through our three-member human meat grinder, but we also knew anger alone would not be enough to get the job done. So we prayed, we poured out our hearts to God, we pleaded for Velora's protection, and we asked God to help us figure out what to do from here.

Rushing in like fools would not help; I knew that. Strang had abundant firepower, a cult full of willing Theo-zombies, and a very particular hostage that we knew he would not hesitate to hurt if he deemed it necessary.

What we needed here was a trap.

"Okay, team, time to put our heads together. We need to trap a rat; so, what do we know?"

"That Strang needs to be whacked."

I grinned. "Thank you for that wise contribution, Aly. I appreciate that. What else do we know? Carrie, what say ye?"

She was silent for a few moments, then closed her eyes and began to speak.

"Strang is careful. He will not leave Velora unattended, lest she run away or someone rescue her before the wedding. So, just snatching her and running is out of the question, I think. He is also very proud, though; if there is anything we can use against him, that may be it."

I narrowed my eyes and smiled a mean, happy little smile. "Proverbs 16:18, 'Pride goeth before destruction, and an haughty spirit before a fall.'"

"Exactly."

"Then we need to help James Strang fall, my dear sisters; we need to help the man fall."

Chapter Twelve

"You sure this will work, Kyle? I mean, why wouldn't he just shoot you and be done with it without all the hassle?"

The concern was thick in Aly's voice. And, truth be told, I knew the risk was very real. I smiled, though. Paying attention to details always tended to pay good dividends, and I had paid very good attention when we were in the home of James Strang.

"It will work. Nothing takes longer than a good chess game, and I guarantee you, Strang believes himself to be an absolute chess master. That set he had on the living room table in his home was ornate, expensive, and used. It was not set up as a display; it had been played, was sitting in the checkmate position, and had been a blowout. Strang beat somebody badly and left it like that, so any visitors would know.

"When I show up and challenge him in front of everybody, he will both view it as an insult and also think I will be a pushover because of my age."

Carrie considered that carefully.

"Are you sure you can beat him? I mean, you have no idea how good he is."

"Well, even though it really isn't necessary for me to beat him, since that will merely be a distraction for you guys, yeah, I am actually pretty confident I can beat him."

They seemed skeptical, so I explained myself.

"Who is the smartest person we know?"

"Dad," they both echoed without the slightest hesitation.

"Correct. And how many games of chess did he beat me in since he taught us?"

"Like, a gajillion or so," Aly giggled.

She was right. And they were really bad beatings. When I was little, it really made me mad; I mean, he showed no mercy whatsoever. Even Mom mildly scolded him about it on more than one occasion.

"Sweetie," he would say, "I intend to make all of my children both tough and smart. When he can beat me, either in fighting or in chess, I will never worry about him again."

I was still way off on the fighting, I knew that. But just a couple of months ago…

"I beat him. If I can beat him, I can beat Strang, 'cause I guarantee you, Dad is better than him. But, like I said, all I really have to do is keep him busy long enough for you two to find and free Velora, get her to wherever Strang keeps his boats, and get her long gone."

The girls nodded with determination.

"Scouting time?"

"Yes, my brainiac sister, scouting time. Let's find Strang's harbor, and then let's rescue Velora."

"Hopefully, we can do all of that in one day; no need to drag things out," said Carrie.

Our beginning task for the day would be simple in theory, but I suspected it would be more difficult in practice. In theory, all we had to do was keep to the shoreline, but just inside the cover of the trees to avoid detection and start making our way around Beaver Island until we found the boats. I was guessing they would be on the eastern side, since across the lake to the east is where most of the "Gentiles" would be for Strang to raid.

I knew that we were currently on the western shore; the sun was just now beginning to rise and peek over the trees from the other side of the island. The question, then, was whether to head north or south to reach the eastern side.

Carrie seemed to read my mind.

"What would Papa say?"

I grinned and adopted his Alabama drawl for the answer: "When in doubt, go south."

Running, we could have gotten to the other side of the island very quickly. We could also have been heard, seen, and caught very quickly. So, keeping about ten yards inside the tree line, we moved as quietly as Black Crow or Rainwater would.[*]

"Nice to have been trained by the best," Carrie whispered.

I nodded ever so slightly, paying attention to every spot I was about to place my foot. Aly was behind me; Carrie, as usual, "had our six."

Our task was daunting. We would need to do what we had not done on day one: namely, avoid being captured by any of Strang's sentries. We also needed to move fast enough to find the harbor, see what boat could be easily commandeered, and then get back to the center of the island to challenge the would-be king.

The pace went reasonably fast; I knew enough from our previous experience to recognize

---

[*] The Night Heroes: The Blade of Black Crow (Vol. 4) and The Night Heroes: When Serpents Rise (Vol. 6)

undisturbed ground when I saw it. And it made sense; Strang would likely see no need to booby-trap the perimeter of his kingdom; his focus would be on protecting his compound. He would, though, doubtless have watchers with eyes on the water facing the mainland, in case of enemy boats sailing that way.

Those watchtowers would be the main things we would need to be alert for.

The breeze seemed to kiss our efforts all morning long. The walking was cool, pleasant, and quiet. About an hour in, though, we came across the first guard tower.

I put my hand and fist up to signal to the girls to stop behind me. Then I pointed through the trees and made sure they saw what I saw. I looked over my shoulder at them, and my eyes got wide. I shook my head back and forth, and my face had the "absolutely not!" look on it. Aly had her slingshot out and was getting ready to let one fly.

Could she hit the dude? Absolutely. Would it cause more harm than good? Double absolutely. At the moment, we needed quiet, not chaos.

I shook my head "no" even more firmly. Aly huffed, glared at me, and pocketed her trusty weapon.

Girls.

Slowly and quietly, I aimed us further back into the trees to loop far around the guard tower. I knew that movement is always the easiest thing to see.

We blew about half an hour getting back on track well on the other side of that first tower. It could not have been more than half a mile, though, before we came upon the next one.

Carrie slipped up beside me.

"We have to be close to the harbor for him to be putting them this near together."

I nodded in agreement, and we once again headed back inland to loop around this tower. I was a bit frustrated; this was slowing us down more than I wanted. But at least we were thus far undetec—

And that is when I heard the click. Why, oh why were we constantly hearing that sound?

"Well, well, well, look what we have here, yet again!" Wilford gloated. His jaw was still swollen a bit from where I laid him out on day one.

I knew this guy had not been skilled enough to track us; he had simply been off in the woods, likely slacking off on whatever task Strang had him doing, and we had walked right by him. He was now standing about fifteen feet behind Carrie and had a pistol in his hand, hanging down by his side. This was nothing more than a case of bad luck…

For him.

"Behold, the filthy Gentiles return," he said dramatically, and then it was mostly, as Aly would put it, "blah blah blahbitty blah," or, as Carrie would put it, he was monologuing.

In front of her, where he could not see, Aly was slowly handing me her slingshot and a metal ball. She had saved me and Carrie both a whole bunch of times with that thing; could I do the same for her and Carrie? If I missed that first shot, we would all be dead, starting with the girls. Carrie was watching, and I knew she knew what was coming.

"…the glorious kingdom of King Strang, Ruler of Heaven and Earth, who…"

With the most imperceptible of movements, I loaded the shot.

"…until such time as all the nations bow…"

I pulled back on the band, slowly but fully.

"…that none are so great and glorious as the people of…"

I whispered a prayer, "Lord, may I borrow my littlest sister's skill set just for a moment, please?"

"…whose dominion shall be forev—"

Like a striking snake, I whipped my hands upward and let the shot fly. Wilford tried to bring his gun up to fire but never got the chance; my shot hit him dead center of his forehead, and he instantly crumpled to the ground, out like a light.

"WHOOOOOOAAAAAAA!!!" Aly scream/whispered, trying not to be heard by anyone else. "Dude, you hit him in the forehead! You never even shoot slingshots; I will never, ever doubt you again. How in the world did you do that?!?"

"We can talk about that later," I said. "You two help me get this guy tied up and gagged so he doesn't cause us any more trouble."

Using supplies from our packs, we quickly got our would-be captor tied to a tree, gagged, and out of commission. Then we covered him with branches and brush and erased any signs of us ever being in the area and left him to his knotty-headed beauty sleep.

I motioned for the girls to follow, and we headed out once again. I only made it a few steps, though, before Aly grabbed me by the arm.

"Kyle, seriously, thank you. I didn't have any idea you even knew how to shoot a slingshot, let alone that perfectly. I have never even seen you practice; how did you manage to pop him right in the forehead?"

I smiled and put both hands on her small shoulders as I faced her. "I was aiming for his chest."

All the color drained from her face. I shrugged and motioned for the girls to follow.

"I'm handing it to Carrie next time," I heard her mumble.

We had to loop around several more guard towers over the next few hours. Finally, with only a couple more hours of daylight left, we found the harbor. There, just across the beach from where we knelt, hiding behind a pile of brush on the edge of the tree line, was a really nice pier (doubtless made with materials they had stolen from "the Gentiles"), and anchored to it were what would pass for a warship in those days and four smaller boats.

The warship would be out of the question for our task; no way could Carrie and Aly handle the sails, rudder, and everything else by themselves. So, it would have to be one of the smaller boats that they commandeered to get themselves and Velora to the mainland and freedom.

That brought up a couple more problems, though. One, if that warship gave chase, they could neither outrun it nor defend themselves against it. Two, all of those boats were heavily guarded.

"We're running kind of thin on time for today, Kyle," Carrie whispered as we all looked across the way and sized up the situation.

"I know, I know," I said with a bit of strain in my voice. I guess I am a lot like Dad; I really hate it when my schedule doesn't work out like I plan. For now, though, we would just have to roll with it, because that big ship had to somehow be put out of commission while appearing to be in perfect working order. Blow it up, like we did in Savannah, and the entire cult would come crashing down on us, with nowhere for us to run. Put a hole in it, and it would be seen and repaired, and our presence would be known.

This was going to take subtlety—and some big gulps of air.

Chapter Thirteen

The time seemed to pass at a snail-like pace as we waited for the sun to disappear below the western sky and darkness to assume its temporary hold on that part of the world. In the meantime, I was watching and memorizing every movement of Strang's dorky disciples. True to form, he had them behaving in a methodical manner well-befitting the military genius he deemed himself to be. On a lone island in Lake Michigan, two of them were marching back and forth like the guardians of the Tomb of the Unknown Soldier.

Irony, that; as we lay there in the year 1852, there actually was no Tomb of the Unknown Soldier yet.

I was also using the black dirt of the island to coat my face and hands and slipping into a long-sleeved, solid-black T-shirt. To paraphrase Yoda, I and the Dark Side were about to become one.

I would need to start my crawl as soon as they passed by each other. I would have to be deathly silent but would also need to hurry. I would have around forty-five seconds to get far enough past them to not be seen, and then I would have to stop for thirty seconds and then start my crawl again. If I could get to the dock and into the water unseen, our plan should work.

The sun finally bid farewell to Michigan for that day. We waited another hour until all was dark and my eyes had adjusted. Then, at just the spot I figured they needed to be, I started crawling out across the sand.

Five seconds, and I was reminding myself to hurry but to also be very quiet.

Ten seconds, and I was in a good crawling groove; forearm, knee, forearm, knee.

Twenty seconds, and I was to their line.

Thirty seconds, and I knew they had made the turn and were heading back, but I could not see that far in the dark.

Forty seconds, and I was frantically hustling to get to my spot.

Forty-five seconds, I stopped dead still and waited.

Fifty seconds, someone stepped on my hand.

I stifled back a scream as my hand mashed down into the sand. I knew that whoever stepped on it probably thought it was just part of the uneven sand or maybe foliage from the trees. I also knew that if I made a sound, they would instantly grab me, and that neither I nor my sisters nor Velora would ever make it home again.

On the other side of me, a foot brushed against my leg on the way by.

In horror, I realized what was happening; it was shift change for the guards. And that meant, even if these two did not accidentally find me, the other two were about to be walking right back in the same direction! There was just about no way one of them was going to miss stepping on me at this rate or seeing me if I got up to run.

Aly, God bless my mischievous little sister, was Johnny on the spot, pulling out what was now an oldie-but-goodie for us. As I looked back, I saw a familiar red dot leap to life and land on the sand between the four guards. I heard them gasp, and one whisper, "Look!" And then, in what would surely have won a *Funniest Home Videos* contest, Aly began to lead them.

Four grown men would slowly approach the dot, and it would dart a few feet to the north, with the men pursuing it. Further, further, further it led them, all the way to the tree line, and to the base of a decent-sized elm tree.

"No way…" I mumbled to myself.

Way. Aly slowly sent that dot up the trunk of the tree, and one of the guards, then the next, then the next, then the next started climbing after it!

I stifled a laugh; we would be talking about these nuts in the trees for a long time.

I had work to do, though, so I left Aly to her fun and resumed my crawl toward the dock. Under a minute later, I was there. I eased silently into the water and pulled myself all the way to the second pylon, where I knew the rope was waiting. I reached up, found the rope, and gently pulled it into the water with me. Finding one end, I did what Dad had taught me to do since childhood: I took a breath, then breathed about half of it out as I sank feet first down into the water.

Blowing out part of my air allowed me to easily sink below the surface. I still had enough air, though, to stay under for maybe thirty seconds.

I pulled myself to the bottom of the pylon and wrapped the rope around it. I could not see, but I could certainly feel; I tied a good, solid knot, then silently came up out of the water under the pier, calmed my racing heart, and took another breath.

I blew half of it out again and sank once more beneath the dark waters of the lake. I swam that rope in loops around several more pylons, tied another knot, and came up for another breath of air.

So far, so good, but now was the hard part.

I took a minute to get my heart and breathing settled down again, then took the very end of the rope and sank beneath the water yet again. Pulling myself frog-style through the murky depths, I found the very back and bottom of the boat; I knew that was where the rudder should be.

Old wooden sailboat-style ships could guide themselves somewhat, but certainly not well, with only sails. So, all of them tended to have an inboard rudder on the back bottom of the ship. They were actually attached in such a way as to make them part of the keel of the boat, meaning, for our purposes, that they weren't going anywhere.

You probably know by now what I had in mind.

I managed to find the rudder, but by that time, I was out of breath. So, I came back to the surface, got a good breath, and dove down again. I found the rudder and then tied the rope around it for all it was worth. Whoever tried to sail that boat out of the harbor was either going to rip the rudder clean off, leaving the boat unable to be steered, or was going to come to a jarring stop until they could figure out what was going on and get the rope cut away.

I resurfaced, took another deep breath, and then dove down again. I did not come up for a good long way; as planned, I was swimming along the shoreline back to the south and would hopefully rendezvous with Carrie and Aly around the bend and out of sight.

An hour later, we three were sitting safely back under the cover of the trees and had built a circular enclosure of loose brush. This allowed us to build a small fire that would not be seen by any prying eyes in any direction. And I needed it; I was soaking wet and freezing cold. The waters of Lake Michigan, in the way Dad would put it, "ain't no joke."

The day had been productive; not as much as we had planned, but we trusted that God was in control of the schedule.

We finally fell asleep. I don't know what my sisters were dreaming about, but I was dreaming of weird human nuts swaying in the breeze of the trees, with giant squirrels climbing their way.

Chapter Fourteen

The day dawned fair and lovely in Michigan; I was kind of getting the feeling that it always did. I stretched, yawned an amazingly oversized yawn, and then plopped my feet onto the floor. The girls were already up, dressed, and sitting on the couch, reading their Bibles.

Within fifteen minutes, I was showered and dressed and sitting on the bed reading my Bible as well. There is absolutely no better way to start the day than with Bible reading and a time of prayer. Soon enough, though, we were all heading down to the lobby for breakfast. We knew this was supposed to be some kind of special day, but we did not yet know what a Frankenmuth was.

We were going to find out.

We were going to be glad we found out.

As we gulped down our eggs and pancakes and bacon, Mom and Dad asked how we slept. That was always an interesting question; technically, the completely correct answer would be "very well and not well at all." But since that would be impossibly difficult to explain, we just went with the "very well" part of it, which was absolutely true. I figured that anytime you could go to sleep in the past and wake up back in your own time was very well indeed.

Once breakfast was done and we had our area completely cleaned up, it was back out to the trusty old Yukon for another trip over to the church. Once again on this day, we all loaded up into the church van with Pastor Todd and his family. I grinned as I noticed some tiny remnants of goldfish crackers on the floor. That was always a really, really good sign for the church; it meant that there were kids, and, therefore, life and a future for the church.

Our trip on that day took just over an hour. We went sixty miles to the north of the church and ended up at... Christmas.

Frankenmuth, as you can probably tell from the name, is a city that has deep German roots. All the buildings, as Dad explained, are Bavarian style. But the highlight of it all is Bronner's Christmas Store.

99

To say the place is huge would be an understatement. The store itself is nearly seven and a half acres! That is nearly enough to fit six football fields inside it. And they have absolutely anything and everything Christmas: decorations, lights, nativity scenes, trees, candy, fudge, clothing, everything.

You could go there in August, in one-hundred-degree weather, and it would take you under three seconds to be in the Christmas spirit.

Mom said she wanted one of the life-sized sleighs; Dad actually said no on that, because she was kidding, but if she had really wanted it, I promise you, it would have been strapped to the top of the Yukon before we left Michigan.

We stayed at Bronner's for several hours and felt like we barely scratched the surface. By then, we were all receiving a pretty important call that let us know our time there was short, though, specifically, the call of lunch, announced by our rumbly stomachs.

A short time later, we found ourselves at another epic place there in Frankenmuth, the Bavarian Inn, for lunch.

If you are ever in that town, do not miss it for anything in the world.

The food was outstanding. The atmosphere made you feel like you were having a meal in Germany during Christmas in the old days.

"This is way cooler than real Germany," Carrie whispered to me. I nodded; considering we almost got trapped there in World War II, I could not disagree with her assessment.

After lunch, we spent some time in the lower level of the Bavarian Inn. Down there, you find gifts and souvenirs and all kinds of food items to buy and take home. And it was there that we had the most entertaining moment of the day.

"You want that? Seriously? That sounds terrible!"

Pastor Todd was standing at a counter with his son, Lincoln, whom we quickly learned was absolutely addicted to Ranch. Not just the dressing; anything and everything that flavor could conceivably be found in or put on.

This, though, this...

"Son, it's literally cotton candy. Do you know how bad Ranch cotton candy is going to be?"

As happens so often, the kid's million-watt smile won the day. Pastor Todd merely shook his head, forked over a few dollars, and said, "This should be entertaining."

The prized and unorthodox cotton candy stayed in its container until we got to the van to head back to the church. That proved to be a mistake; when he opened it in the small confines of the van, the smell was... bad. I mean, like, horrible.

"Uggh, are you seriously going to put that in your mouth?" Sister Todd asked incredulously.

Yes, in fact, he was, and he did. Worse still, kind of like a train wreck, all of us knew that we were going to have to try it as well, or we would regret the lost opportunity. It felt kind of like that old commercial where one raccoon is smelling something and looks at his friend raccoon and says, "Yuck, this smells awful; try it!"

You know how sometimes something smells terrible but actually tastes really good?

This was not one of those times.

Our next stop was at a gas station to get drinks to wash the awful taste out of our mouths.

An hour later, we were back at the church, loading up into our vehicle, and heading back to the hotel for just a bit. We would rest some or work some as was needed. I knew we would also be getting a bit of supper before church, which we did, once again at the Culver's.

And then it was on to the church for another night of the meeting.

As with all of the previous services, the singing before the preaching was just so awesome; it really sometimes feels like you are about to go to Heaven while you are singing about it.

Finally, though, Dad was back in the pulpit. This time, he preached a message called "What's So Great About the Great Commission."

It is taken from Matthew 28:19-20, where Jesus told His followers what they were to do after He went back to Heaven. Basically, every believer up into our day and beyond is to be winning souls to Christ all over the world, baptizing them, and then teaching them all that the Bible teaches.

God really is serious about seeing people saved, seeing them follow Him, and seeing them obey the Word.

There was a good crowd around the altar during the invitation, and I suspected that many of them were praying that God would help them to fulfill the Great Commission in such a way that God would be pleased with what He saw in them.

We ourselves were in that crowd.

Not too long later, the glow of all of that was subsiding; we were heading back to the hotel, Mom and Dad for a night of rest, and the girls and I for another confrontation with James Strang.

Chapter Fifteen

I could feel myself panicking; the giant horse was airborne and was going to land right on me! If it did, I knew I was dead. I braced for impact—then out of nowhere, some guy in a long robe and pointy hat came charging in from the side, hit that horse broadside, and sent it sprawling off the scene.

I knew I had to get up; I couldn't, though, and I wasn't sure why. I looked down and, in horror, saw that I had no arms or legs, just a stubby, plastic-looking tubular body!

I rolled over just as an entire castle landed where I had just been. And then, the most regal-looking lady I have ever seen swooped in, smashed the castle, and helped me up.

"My queen!" I said in adoration.

"I will never let you forget that you called me that, Kyle."

Oh boy.

I opened my right eye; the early morning sun of Beaver Island was just starting to check in for the day. Carrie was standing over me, grinning, and extending a hand to me. Aly was beside her, doing the same.

I reached up and grabbed their hands, and they pulled me to my feet.

"Dreaming of chess, I presume?" the Conductor said dryly.

"Yes, sir, I suppose so. Not sure if that's a good thing or a bad thing, but it is a thing, either way."

He nodded, then motioned back over his shoulder with his head.

"Strang is in the camp. Velora is somewhere tucked away, but I am not certain quite where; the devil's forces are thick, keeping her hidden from view."

We knew what he meant by the devil's forces. Like Paul said, we wrestle not against flesh and blood.

I kind of smiled at the irony of that. My sisters and I very much did wrestle against flesh and blood. But the truth of Paul's words was that behind that flesh and blood, there was always a spiritual war raging, a world of angels and demons that we could not see, and our physical efforts could therefore only make a difference when powered by spiritual things like prayer.

"Are you all ready for the day?"

"We will be in just a minute, sir," and I knew that he knew what we meant.

We all knelt down in the sand there by the waters of Beaver Island.

"Lord, Velora's note was a cry for help from us and from Heaven. You sent us here at least for her, so please help us to succeed. Help me not to be overconfident in myself, but please help none of us to be afraid, either. When we leave here, may the king have been dethroned and knocked off of his private little playing board. We pray this in Jesus' name, amen."

We stood to our feet, looked around, and, as usual, the Conductor was gone.

"Gabriel or Dr. Who?" Carrie inquired with a grin.

I didn't answer, I just smiled and shrugged. We had pretty much decided on the angel thing a long time ago.

The next few minutes were a whirlwind of preparation. The girls had pulled their new "makeup" out of their bags and were camouflaging their faces and arms. By the time they were done, I had to admit that it was a really admirable job; they were going to fade into the wooded terrain perfectly.

"I guess all those hours in front of a mirror have not been in vain," I said. "In vanity, but not in vain."

"Don't be a hater; be an appreciator," Aly said with mock elegance.

We went over the plans for the day one final time, then parted ways. I never liked doing that; I always wanted to be right beside my sisters to protect them from any harm. Nonetheless, I also knew that they are super capable, smart, and brave, and anyone who crossed them was in for more than he bargained for.

Carrie and Aly were looping a bit to the southeast back in the trees of Beaver Island. They would be stealthy and smooth as they snuck in the back door, as it were.

I was going to be making myself very well known as I headed right into the teeth of the lion; this would draw attention to me and away from them. It would also (hopefully) keep me from getting shot, since I would not appear to be sneaking in.

Walking through any woods or desert, I have the ability to move noiselessly. This time, though, I chose noise. I walked heavily, kept to the well-trodden path that would take me to Strang—and I sang.

I have an okay voice; not great, but okay. Dad says I will have a solid bass voice by the time all of my growing is done. But today, I was not giving a concert; I was asking for attention.

So, after walking a few hundred yards, I sang, and I sang loudly.

"Marvelous grace of our loving Lord, grace that exceeds our sin and our guilt! Yonder on Calvary's mount outpoured, there where the blood of the Lamb was spilt...

"Grace, grace, God's grace, grace that will pardon and cleanse within; grace, grace, God's grace, grace that is greater than all our sin.

"Sin and despair like the sea waves cold, threaten the soul within infinite loss; grace that is greater, yes, grace untold, points to the refuge, the mighty cross.

"Grace, grace, God's grace, grace that will pardon and cleanse within; grace, grace, God's grace, grace that is greater than all our sin.

"Dark is the stain that we cannot hide, what can avail to wash it away? Look! There is flowing a crimson tide; whiter than snow you may be today...

"Grace, grace, God's grace,
grace that will pardon and cleanse
within; grace, grace, God's grace,
grace that is greater than all our sin.

"Marvelous infinite mat—"

Click.

I sighed; there was that sound again.

I stood very still and just waited. It took less than ten seconds for me to be surrounded by men and weapons. And this was good; it meant all eyes were on me, not on Carrie and Aly.

"What can I do for you, Gentlemen?" I asked pleasantly.

"You can stop singing your heresy, just to begin with," came the angry, nasally response from the thin man who now stepped directly in front of me. He looked very much like a weasel who had been stretched into a human.

I stifled back a laugh at that thought; weasel bullets would kill just as quickly as any others.

"Heresy? What heresy?" I said pleasantly. "You mean Jesus dying to pay for all of our sins and then offering us salvation by grace apart from any works on our part?"

"That's exactly what I mean, you filthy Gentile!"

"Ohhhh, okay," I replied matter-of-factly. "I guess I just have a lot to learn. Fortunately, King

Strang is here, right? Why don't you just take me right on to him? I actually have a bit of a gift for him anyway, something for his impending nuptials."

The men looked at each other and seemed to be a bit confused, so I helped them out. "Nuptials means wedding."

"We know what it means!" a porky little dude with a beard shouted angrily.

"Of course you do, Gimli. So, how's about taking me to see the good king? He surely won't like it if his gift doesn't arrive."

My clearly inept captors put their heads together and whispered things over for a minute. Then the lead guy turned to me abruptly and said, "Move," while nodding in the direction of the camp.

I smiled and set off walking. I was flanked by several to my left and my right, and had a good contingent behind me as well. I felt kind of like the munchkins were taking me to see the Wizard of Oz, and I already knew about the guy behind the curtain.

Hey, this is Carrie. I'll pick the story up from here. Aly and I were silently praying as we made our way through the trees. We knew Kyle was taking a big risk for us; the least we could do was battle in prayer for him.

The day had just a hint of coolness as we made our way stealthily through the trees. We were going slow, way slower than we were capable of. But we knew that we had to get all the way to the back of the camp without being seen or heard if any of us or Velora had a chance.

For all the sarcasm that I give Kyle, much of which he richly deserves, I really missed him right at this moment. I knew he was way better in the woods than me or Aly.

Maybe it was because I was thinking of that that I was careful enough not to get snagged by the trap Strang and his men had set for whoever might be coming by that way.

Beside me, Aly was about to take a step, and I put my arm out and stopped her. She knew better than to make any sounds, so as she looked over at me, I pointed down toward the ground in front of us and mouthed the word, *"Look."*

She had to look pretty hard; anyone would. When she saw it, I saw her eyes get big; there was a thin, nearly invisible string, right about calf level in front of us. As she looked at me again, I made the motion of getting yanked up in the air. She understood; she and I were both there when Rain Water* caught Kyle in the same kind of trap.

Aly made a scissor motion with her fingers, but I shook my head no. Knowing where this trap was could actually be an advantage for us in a pursuit. So, we carefully backed away and made a loop about thirty feet around that entire area.

The rest of the trip to the camp was relatively uneventful, but slow, oh, so slow. The last mile, just to be safe, we crawled on our hands and knees, making sure not to break a single twig or rustle a single leaf.

After what seemed like absolutely forever, we were through the village and behind the house of James Strang. There, we had a vantage point across the compound to the front gate.

We arrived at that vantage point at the exact moment we saw Kyle escorted into the camp by Strang's armed entourage.

---

* The Night Heroes: When Serpents Rise (Vol. 6)

Chapter Sixteen

"All hail the king!" they shouted.

"All hail the king indeed!" came the reply of everyone in camp. We could see everyone quickly gathering around; Kyle's presence was immediately drawing attention.

Kyle was jostled to the very center of the compound, and, at that exact moment, James Strang came out on the balcony of his house.

"Why are you here again, Gentile? Did I not make my expectations on that matter clear enough the first time around?"

Everything in camp was silent enough that we could have heard a pin drop. Strang had asked a question, and Kyle was expected to answer.

"I am actually here on what should probably be a private matter; I have no desire to embarrass you in front of anyone."

Oooooh! That was genius! Kyle was boxing this guy in; if he brought Kyle inside, everyone would think that Strang did indeed have something about which to be embarrassed. I knew that his pride would never allow that.

I also knew there was one more layer to that trap about to be laid.

"I have nothing to hide, nor anything about which to be embarrassed; state your peace here, out in the open, for everyone, boy."

Even from here, I could see the hint of a smile on Kyle's face. He was reeling this guy in, and he knew it.

"It really isn't a serious matter; actually, I find it to be quite an enjoyable matter. When we were in your home, I could not help but notice the lovely and ornate chess set on your table. It struck me as interesting because you believe yourself to be a king, and a king who cannot be taken. I believe that you are neither a king nor nearly as brilliant as you make yourself out to be to these, your gullible followers.

"I'm here to challenge you to a game of chess, which, since you have nothing to be embarrassed over, you clearly will not mind doing in public. What say you have some of your guys bring the table and the chess set out, we'll set it up right here in the center of camp, where everyone can watch, and you can prove how brilliant you are.

"Unless, of course, you're afraid that you might lose to a boy, and a 'Gentile' boy at that."

Boom. Kyle had him; there's no way he would say no now.

He didn't even hesitate.

"Bring it." He said without ever taking his eyes off of Kyle. His voice was cold; I knew his temper was the exact opposite, though he was not showing it.

Four men immediately rushed up the stairs and into the house behind Strang. In a matter of moments, they had carried the table down into the courtyard and had also, very carefully, carried the chess set. They set the table up, put a chair on either side of it, and set the chess set in the center as Strang descended the steps. Regally, he crossed the courtyard, as his followers parted to let him through as if he were Moses walking through the Red Sea.

Kyle sat down, and Strang sat down across from him.

"Let us begin," Strang said as he reached for a pawn.

"There's our cue," I whisper to Aly. "Set your watch; we have one hour."

Hey everybody, this is Kyle, I'll pick the story back up from here.

For those who do not know, chess is a really elaborate, strategy-filled game. Let me give you a quick rundown of how it goes.

There are thirty-two pieces on a chessboard, sixteen on each side. They are set up in two lines. The first line, in front of the important pieces, consists of eight pawns. They can only move one spot at a time, except for their very first move, where they have the option of moving two spaces. They can also only move straightforward, unless they are taking another piece, in which they can move one diagonal space.

If they make it to the end of the board, they can be switched out for any other of your pieces that have been taken.

On each back corner, there is a rook, sometimes called a castle. They can move in a straight line forward or side to side as far as they want until there is another piece in their way.

Beside each of the rooks, there is a knight, sometimes called a horse. They move in an L shape, two squares in one direction, and then one more square either to the left or the right of that. They are the only pieces that can jump other pieces.

Beside the knights are the bishops. They can move diagonally across the board as far as the path is clear. Beside one of the bishops is a queen, placed on her own color. She is the most powerful piece on the board and can move in any direction as far as she wants until she comes to another piece.

Finally, each side has a king, placed beside the queen. The king, honestly, is kind of lame; he can only move one space, though he can do so in any direction. His only job is not to be taken; when he is placed in a position where he cannot avoid being taken, it is called checkmate, and the game is over.

Like I said, pretty elaborate. Compared to checkers, chess requires much more thinking, scheming, and planning.

Strang and I were beginning to move our pieces across the board. I knew that, under the circumstances, he was going to be very aggressive, as many chess players are, and try to end me in as few moves as possible. I, though, had the exact opposite plan in mind: first of all, because of what our real goal was in all of this, and secondly, because of how my Dad taught me to play, and his grandfather, the Tulane University chess champ, taught him to play.

My strategy was to win by attrition. That simply means to wear down an opponent and take all of the resources until they can no longer fight. So, while Strang was trying his best to get to my king as quickly as possible, I was calmly moving pieces around the board to take every little small piece of his that I possibly could.

When he slid a bishop way across the board and took one of my knights, I gulped a little bit; I did not see that coming, and it hurt. Much of my strategy revolved around the use of those two knights.

"A bit careless, are we?" Strang said sarcastically.

I scanned the new landscape of the board, evaluating the defenses I had in place for just such an eventuality. It only took me a couple of seconds to find what I needed to find.

"We?" I asked pleasantly. "I think you mean 'you.'"

I smiled, then slid one of my bishops across the board to take a pawn. And while that may not seem like a good exchange, it was, in fact, a great exchange, because it meant that no matter what he did, with my next move, I would take either his rook or one of his knights.

I saw Strang's face stiffen, and his hand and arm tense up a bit. He was not expecting that; in fact, he was clearly not expecting much of a contest at all.

His problem, not mine.

To his credit, the man was a good strategist. I knew that not just because of the adjustments he made after that, but also because of the change in conversation. As soon as he hit that rough spot, which resulted in me taking one of his rooks, he began to talk theology, figuring to divert my attention from the board.

Fortunately, that is also something I was very much anticipating and, in fact, hoping for. My Dad has taught all of us the Bible very well; if this went as well as I hoped, maybe some of his followers would be able to see through his lies and would come to know Christ.

"You do know that your precious Jesus and Satan are actually brothers, don't you? You revere him as a God, but he is no more of God than I will one day be, and that you could be, if you chose to come to the truth."

"I actually don't know that," I said, "mostly because it's completely not true. Speaking of Jesus, John 1:1-3 says, 'In the beginning was the Word, and the Word was with God, and the Word was God. The same was in the beginning with God. All things were made by him; and without him was not any thing made that was made.' But when it comes to Satan, Ezekiel 28:15 says, 'Thou wast perfect in thy ways from the day that thou wast created, till iniquity was found in thee.'

"So, Jesus never was created; He created all things, and Satan was one of those created things. Mind you, he was created perfect, and chose to sin, becoming the devil. But there has never been a moment in all of time or eternity when those two were brothers. Nor will there ever be a moment that you or I or anyone else are a god of any kind; 1 Timothy 2:5 says, 'For there is one God, and one mediator between God and men, the man Christ Jesus.' "

I took a breath, reached for the board again, and said, "Nor will you ever have this bishop again in this game," as I landed on it with my remaining knight.

Strang grimaced but quickly recovered, sending his queen across the board into one of my rooks.

"Your theology is as poor as your defense, boy," he snapped. "You Gentiles and your weakness, your peddling of grace rather than acceptance of your responsibilities, renders you senseless."

"Well, we finally have something to agree on," I said pleasantly. "I am indeed weak. Like Paul, in my flesh, there is no good thing. We are so weak, in fact, that we know better than to try to work our way into Heaven, much less into godhood. Because of that, we are more than willing to simply and gladly receive the grace that you so mock and despise.

"Ephesians 2:8-9 says, 'For by grace are ye saved through faith; and that not of yourselves: it is the gift of God: Not of works, lest any man should boast.' "

Things got much tighter on the board after that point. For a while, no more big pieces were taken, though I was systematically eliminating Strang's pawns. The theology debate continued; the game continued—I just hoped that behind the scenes, Carrie and Aly were having good success finding and freeing Velora. Otherwise, we were all going to end up being taken.

Chapter Seventeen

Hey everybody, this is Carrie. I'll pick the story up again at this point.

While Kyle and Strang were doing battle on the board there in the courtyard, Aly and I, as silently as ninjas, were sneaking into one building after another to try and find Velora. Obviously, Strang's home had been first, but she was not there.

I looked at my watch and started to panic; we only had ten minutes left!

"Carrie, we've got to find her, but we've looked everywhere!"

"I know, I know!" I hissed back.

When it hit me, I put my face in my hands and said, "Oh, man…"

"What? What is it?"

"We have to get back to Strang's place, right away."

"But we've already searched it!" she said.

"Not thoroughly enough. Trust me. Let's go."

Keeping out of sight, we raced back around the perimeter of the camp to get in behind Strang's home one more time. Then, as before, we climbed the tree hanging over the corner of the back deck, dropped out of the branch onto it, and once again came in through the back door.

We quickly, but as quietly as the moon in the night sky, made our way inside, and I veered to the wall on the right and started running my hands over it.

"What are you doing?" Aly hissed.

"Give me a second," I said as I kept feeling the wall.

"Bingo," I said. "Step back."

Aly stepped back, and I pushed hard on the edge of the board my hand was on. Instantly, the wall began to separate in the middle and open into the room.

Aly gasped; the wall opened wide enough for a person to walk in, and behind it, tied to the real wall and gagged, was Velora.

As quick as a flash, I had my knife out (Dad's rule; guy or girl, never be without a knife) and had cut Velora free. Then we were rushing quietly back to the deck, to the tree to climb down—and to one more needed task before we raced for freedom.

Hey again, this is Kyle; I'll pick the story back up from here.

I obviously had no way of knowing what was going on with Carrie and Aly; I was having to just trust them to get their part of the job done.

And I did; anyone underestimating any girl is dumb, but to underestimate my sisters would be, in the words of my Dad, "as dumb as a bag of hair." They had proven themselves time and time again, and I knew they would come through this time, too. And that left me the luxury to pay attention to just two things: the board and my watch.

"You are decent enough at this, boy, though clearly no match for me. Perhaps you should stay on and let me teach you both chess and theology."

As he said that, I closed my eyes and grinned, oh, so slightly. Without even looking, I knew that he was about to slide his bishop across the board and take my queen. So, why was I smiling at that?

Because that is exactly the bait I had intentionally dangled in front of him—bait that I knew he would find irresistible.

I heard the piece slide across the board and opened my eyes to see him lifting my queen and putting her off to the side of the table.

"That was careless, Boy. You now have a problem; you are without your queen."

I nodded as if in agreement. Then I calmly reached up, took my rook, and moved it into a spot that his move had left open.

"I have one problem, but you have three. One, checkmate. Two, I have lost my queen on the chessboard, but you have lost the intended queen of your weird little kingdom. And, three...your armory is on fire."

Everything broke loose at that moment. Strang whipped his head around toward the edge of camp, and sure enough, a building was on fire. As planned, Carrie and Aly had taken steps to eliminate the powder and weapons with which the Strangites had attacked innocent people a couple of nights ago, had doubtless done so many times in the past, and doubtless would continue doing so if given the opportunity.

Strang screamed, "Sound the alarm!" and a huge bell at the other side of the camp began to ring out across the island. This, of course, is exactly what we needed to get the men away from the dock and boats so that we could get off the island.

The second Strang screamed, and everyone rushed toward the fire to put it out. I flipped the table over and ran the other direction. It was good that I did; shots rang out, and I knew they were meant for me. Instead, they thumped into the table or went wide of me.

I rushed into the trees, making for the shoreline where I knew the girls intended to meet me. There was no more sneaking and going slow; I was moving on, and I knew that, wherever they were, they were as well.

I had very much hoped not to have any pursuit, though I suspected that ultimately, fire or no, I would. Sure enough, out of the corner of my eye, I saw Earnest coming like a goofy, skinny, pasty-white savage.

I turned to meet him but never got the chance.

"Yaaaaiiiiiiiii!" I heard him scream as his feet suddenly whipped out from underneath him, and he was yanked into the air by them.

"Nice..." I said as I grinned. Then, even though I really wanted to stay for a minute and mock the fact that he was caught in his own trap, I took off running for the shore again. I arrived a few minutes later, just in time to see Carrie, Aly, and Velora untying one of the rowboats. I rushed to join them—then had the breath completely knocked out of me.

I hadn't even seen this dude coming before he dove shoulder-first into my side.

"Kyle!"

I couldn't answer Aly's scream; I could not even catch my breath, he had hit me so hard. I looked up and quickly sized things up, and it was bad. This dude was huge, strong, angry, and had his fist rared back to punch my lights out.

And I couldn't do a thing about it.

As it turns out, I didn't have to.

Whack! came the solid thud to the back of his head. He fell off, doubled over, holding his head where one of the girls, not sure which, had smashed him with one of the paddles. But they were not done, not by a long shot. As I tried desperately (for his sake) to catch my breath, the three of them commenced to beating the ever-living daylights out of him with their paddles. They whacked his head, his legs, his arms, but they mostly seemed to be whacking his posterior again and again and again.

I kind of suspected that may be intentional.

Finally, I caught my breath enough to say, "Hold! That's enough; this guy is going to join a monastery when he heals up, so he never has to see Strang, or a boat paddle, or a woman ever again."

They helped me to my feet, and we headed to the boats.

And as soon as we pushed away from the dock, lightning split the sky and thunder immediately pounded our ears.

"Good grief," I said, "why can none of this be easy?"

The next few hours were bad—really bad. All we had to do was get Velora to the mainland and back to her parents, and she would be free. Instead, we found ourselves fighting for our lives as if we were the disciples on the Sea of Galilee.

I really didn't even have to ask if this was coincidental; I knew that it wasn't. The devil does not let any captives go free easily and has not lost any of his diabolical power since the disciples fought their own demonic storm in Mark 4.

The storm was blowing us south, when we wanted to go east. We had no way to stop it; our oar-power was no match for the gale.

"Everybody just hold on!" I screamed, trying desperately to be heard. It really felt like every demon and devil of Hell was in the middle of the storm, trying to pound us to the bottom of Lake Michigan.

And there would be no Gordon Lightfoot to sing our story, because no one would even know about it if we went down.

Chapter Eighteen

I really am glad that, in the words of Hebrews 13:8, Jesus Christ is the same yesterday, today, and forever. I say that because I was praying hard, and I knew my sisters, at least, were doing so as well, and God came through for us. Our little boat, finally, after hours of being tossed on the waves, washed up on the shore of some other little island in Lake Michigan.

Carrie's guess was that, since we had been going south, it was probably one of the uninhabited Fox Islands.

As soon as the boat rode up onto the beach, the storm stopped as if someone had simply flipped a switch.

"Yeah, same to you, buddy," I said, and I knew my sisters knew I was directing that at whatever little devil had been behind the storm.

I crawled out of the boat, then helped Velora and my sisters out as well. Quickly, we built a shelter and a fire back in the trees; being cold and wet is really, really dangerous.

In an hour or so, we were pretty well dried off—and had an issue to deal with.

"Thank you for coming back for me; somehow, I felt like I could trust you all to do so."

I simply nodded as if to say, "You're welcome." Then I actually did speak.

"Velora, we aren't quite out of the woods yet. I cannot explain this, so you will just have to trust me, okay? My sisters and I have to go away for a while, but we will be back, I promise. And you will need us to be back for at least two— maybe three reasons.

"First of all, we obviously still have to get you back to the mainland and to your parents. Secondly, Strang will be coming after you; losing his intended queen is quite the embarrassment and could cost him his so-called kingdom if people begin to question his rule and ability. And three, on the maybe part, I know you have heard all kinds of inaccurate things about Jesus, so I want to know if you actually know Him as you should. Do you understand that He is the Son of God, and that that is what He has always been? Do you understand that He was born of a virgin, and that He lived a perfect life, and that He died on Calvary for you, and that He rose again the third day? Do you understand that salvation is only by grace through placing your faith in Him?"

She was silent for a moment.

"Strang told me many things about Jesus, pretty much all of them exactly the opposite of what you just stated. My parents never really spoke of Him at all. So, no, I guess not."

"I suspected as much."

I reached into my pack and pulled out my Bible, which, as always, was in a waterproof bag, just in case.

"Hole up quietly here for tonight. Read the gospel of John. My sisters and I will be back tomorrow, I promise. Got all that?"

"Yes… yes, I do," she said seriously.

"Good. Now, let me pray over you before we go, okay?"

And then I prayed.

"Lord Jesus, true King of Heaven and Earth, I commit Velora to Your hands for safekeeping on this night. Thank You for giving us escape from Beaver Island, and thank You for keeping us safe across the wild waves. Please protect her and hide her from view on this night, and bring us back tomorrow so that we may finish the job and get her home. All of this I pray in Your precious name, amen."

Chapter Nineteen

The next day, we found that we were in for one of the greatest treats any of us Warners could ever hope to experience. We would be going, of all places, to Lake Michigan, not for adventure, but for rock hunting purposes. We would be looking for Petoskey stones, which are found mostly there on the shores of Lake Michigan.

Petoskey stones are really cool; they are basically conglomerations of fossilized coral, specifically, tightly packed, six-sided corallites. They are really pretty and really unique.

After breakfast, we Warners, the pastor and his family, and Brother Josh and his family loaded up and headed that way. It took us a bit over three hours, so we ate a quick bite of lunch when we got there.

We knew we would only have a couple of hours to hunt for the rocks, but it would be worth it.

It was kind of odd, really, putting my hand down into the waters of Lake Michigan on the edge of the shore and realizing that was the same water we were dealing with in 1852 at night, and the same water that God put there in place either from the Garden of Eden or from the time immediately after Noah's flood.

Carrie and Aly came up beside me as we hunted, and I finally got to speak with them about last night.

"You guys really came through. Nice job, as always."

"Thanks," they both said in unison. But Aly still wanted to talk about it; I could tell that from her "how did you do it" face.

"So, my genius elder sister, spill the tea. How did you know Velora was behind that wall?"

"Simple, really," Carrie said, "which makes me kick myself that I missed it the first time around and almost cost us everything. What was hanging on that wall?"

"A picture of Strang in his Spirit Halloween king costume," Aly said in her standard mocking voice.

"Correct. And where, exactly, on that wall, was the portrait of the man who believes himself to be the one that the entire universe revolves around?"

I saw Aly's eyes widen.

"It wasn't in the dead center of the wall where he would definitely have put it; it was off-center to the right! He couldn't put it in the center because the wall comes apart to let people in or out!"

Carrie took a small bow.

"Nice, Big Brain, nice," I said with admiration.

The day was beautiful once again, and all of us found several very pretty specimens to keep. And then it was back into the church van, and a three-hour nap for me and my sisters as we headed back to Oxbow Lake Baptist Church.

When we arrived, Dad woke us up, we said our goodbyes for now, and we headed back to the hotel to freshen up before church. Then it was through a Chick-fil-A and back to church for the final night of the meeting.

The last night of a meeting is always sort of bittersweet. We had made some great friends and always hated to say goodbye.

As Dad got up to preach, he had everyone open their Bibles to John 1, and, after reading it, he preached a message that I have heard many times before, "The Wonder of the Word." And I am glad that he did; it is a message all about Who and what Jesus is. John really clearly drove home the fact that Jesus has always been, and has always been God. Contrary to what Strang and his followers believe and teach, Jesus did not have to become God; He was always equally as much God as God the Father Himself.

Dad really loves Jesus and wants everyone to know how awesome He is.

We hung around for a good while after the meeting, and I knew that no one really wanted to say goodbye. But the good thing, as a Christian, is that we never actually do say goodbye. Every time we leave, it is really more like "see you later," because we know that, either here, or in Heaven, we will see each other later.

We did eventually have to go, though, and we Warners all hoped we would get to come back again, because we really liked the pastor and his family and the entire church.

We also had to go, though, because we had exactly one more night in which to deal with Strang and get Velora home.

Chapter Twenty

When we awoke the next morning in 1852, we were on the new island. The beach was littered with debris from the night before. The storm had really been a rough one, though we already knew that from experience.

"So, one more day, and Strang will be coming. He is furious and fearful; his followers are already murmuring at his seeming weakness, thanks to you. Are you ready?"

"Not yet, sir, but we will be shortly," I replied with a smile. "We need to pray, and then we need to prepare a welcome for the king with the now-tarnished crown."

The edge of his mouth eased upward in a friendly grin. "Good. Velora is still asleep where you left her. Go get it done."

We prayed, then got right to it. I knew we had two big tasks for the day, one with huge here-and-now value and one with priceless eternal value.

I had Carrie go wake Velora and bring her to us.

"You came back," she said sweetly.

"Believers in Christ keep their word," I replied.

The next few hours were a beehive of activity. Our first task was tearing the boat apart; we were going to need the wood to make a hiding place in the sand for the girls. If we had it our way, we were about to pull the ultimate bait and switch on Strang and company.

Once we were ready, I looked across the waves and saw nothing but water, and that was good; we needed to handle the eternal stuff while we had the time.

"Everyone, huddle up," I said. And then, seeing the strange look on Velora's face at my twenty-first-century terminology, I said, "Everyone, come over here and sit down, please."

Once everyone was seated, I said, "Velora, did you read the gospel of John?"

"I did," she answered, and I thought I saw a tear forming in her eyes as she let her short words trail off.

"What did you think?"

She hesitated as if trying to find the right words.

"I think... I think, um, Jesus is not what I thought. I mean, one minute He is making the entire universe, and the next minute He is kneeling down to wash the dirty feet of fishermen. He was the King, yet He wore a crown of thorns rather than a crown of gold. He died, yet He lives. He was holy, yet He told a sinful woman, 'Neither do I condemn thee: go, and sin no more.'

"He could have condemned the world, but instead came to save those who would simply believe. I think… I think I would very much like to really know Him."

"You can," I replied with absolute confidence. "2 Peter 3:9 says that He is not willing that any should perish, but that all should come to repentance. If you will repent of your sin as Jesus said in Luke 13:3, confess Him as your Lord and believe that He raised from the dead as Romans 10:9-10 says, and call on Him to save you like Romans 10:13 says, you will be saved. Would you like to do that?"

A few moments later, an unwilling would-be queen of a creepy cult leader became a princess, a daughter of the King of kings.

We cried with her, my sisters hugged her, and Aly said, "Welcome, new sister. Now, buckle up, because even though you won't have a clue what this means, you are about to be a temporary Night Hero as well. Let's go kick some Strang booty."

We had seen what Strang and his men could do with a bunch of weapons and powder. Now, though, they would hopefully be coming mostly unarmed and in row boats, if my boat-breaker trap had worked like I planned.

As soon as I saw the rowboats coming, I knew that it had.

I knew he could not hear me from that huge distance across the water. Nonetheless, I grinned and said, "Aww, did the Burglar King lose his whopper? That's a shame, a real shame. So come on in, Strang Bean, let us cook you really good before we leave."

"Wow, Kyle, that is some seriously good pun work," Carrie said with mock admiration. "Now, what say we get ready for the welcome party?"

We headed to our stations and waited.

About twenty minutes later, the boats rowed ashore.

"Velora! Boy! Impertinent little girls! Come out immediately, and I shall mix my wrath with mercy; make me hunt for you, and you shall

all drink of the wine of my wrath without mixture!"

He was really, really hot. And that was good; angry people tend to make stupid decisions and not pay attention.

A dozen men were with him. Thirteen little piggies for us to take to market, as it were.

"I'm here, Strang," I said as I stepped out into the open. "You couldn't catch me when I left with your girl, mostly because you are old and weak and slow and stooooopid." I really dragged that word out: I wanted him humiliated and super-angry. "So, would you like to try again? Come and get me, guy who lost all of the real Mormons to Brigham Young!"

Buddy, I saw fire in that dude's eyes. He screamed like a banshee and tore out after me with all of his men right behind him.

What he never saw was Velora and my sisters pushing their sand-covered boards up and rising from the beach behind them once they were past.

He also did not see me do a baseball slide into another hole a hundred yards into the trees and cover myself with the bush I had ripped up and set there for that purpose.

They went whizzing by, still screaming and cursing.

I got up and made like The Flash, getting back to the beach where the girls were waiting.

Then we simply set fire to all but one of their boats and rowed away in it, leaving them stranded, hopefully forever.

But not before Aly used a stick to draw a girl's face in the sand, sticking her tongue out at them.

Historical Epilogue

James Strang and the Strangites were very real. They were such troublemakers that the United States government sent warships to Beaver Island to apprehend him! Nonetheless, he was such a smooth talker that he represented himself at trial—and won.

His own disgruntled followers eventually assassinated him.

And if you want to know more about the history and beliefs of the Mormons, you can check out the classic in the field, *Kingdom of the Cults*, by Walter Martin.

Other Books in the Night Heroes Series

Cry from the Coal Mine (Vol 1)
Free Fall (Vol 2)
Broken Brotherhood (Vol 3)
The Blade of Black Crow (Vol 4)
Ghost Ship (Vol 5)
When Serpents Rise (Vol 6)
Moth Man (Vol 7)
Runaway (Vol 8)
Terror by Day (Vol 9)
Winter Wolf (Vol 10)
Desert Heat (Vol 11)
Deadline (Vol 12)
The Sword and the Iron Curtain (Vol 13)

Other Fiction

Zak Blue: Falcon Wing
Zak Blue: Enter the Maelstrom

Other Books by Dr. Wagner

Colossians: The Treasures of Deity
Daniel: Breathtaking
Ephesians: The Treasures of Family
Esther: Five Feasts and the Fingerprints of God

Galatians: Treasures of Liberty
Hosea: Love When It Matters Most
James: The Pen and the Plumb Line
Joel, Amos, Obadiah: Turmoil Among the
Nations
Jonah: A Story of Greatness
Nehemiah: A Labor of Love
Philippians: The Treasures of Joy
Proverbs Vol 1: Bright Light from Dark Sayings
Proverbs Vol 2: Bright Light from Dark Sayings
The Revelation: Ready or Not
Romans: Salvation from A-Z
Ruth: Diamonds in the Darkness

Beyond the Colored Coat
From Footers to Finish Nails
Learning Not to Fear the Old Testament
Marriage Makers/Marriage Breakers
I'm Saved! Now What???
Don't Muzzle the Ox
Why Christmas?

Devotionals

DO Drops Vol. 1
DO Drops Vol. 2
DO Drops Vol. 3
DO Drops Vol. 4
DO Drops Vol. 5
DO Drops Vol. 6
DO Drops Vol. 7
DO Drops Vol. 8
DO Drops Vol. 9
DO Drops Vol 10
DO Drops Vol 11
DO Drops Vol 12
DO Drops Vol 13